Whole Lotta Peaches

Peaches Monroe's Diary

BOOK #2 of 4

ANGIE PEPPER

Chapter 1

Before the world could meet their new favorite underwear model, I had to pose for the pictures. And before I could pose for the pictures, I had to sit through hours of hair and makeup.

All those long, quiet hours in the chair did something to me. I got so bored that I actually tried meditating.

I phoned Nisha daily from LA—the city where the photos were being taken—and reported in to her. To say she was thrilled about me meditating would be an understatement. My best friend was unemployed now, so she took on the full-time duty of teaching me how to be more like her. She provided meditation tips, ideas for mantras, and way, way, way too much enthusiasm.

But you don't want to hear about my meditation practice.

You want to know what happened when Dalton Deangelo arrived at the house party, then walked into the kitchen to find me smooching Adrian Stromquist.

The first thing Dalton said was, "Who's this supposed to be?"

Adrian pulled away. "Hi there," he said. "I'm just an old friend. Peaches and I went to school together." He held up the script. "We weren't actually kissing. We were doing a scene read from this script, *Waterfall*. Fantastic movie, by the way. I haven't read the whole thing, but there's some good stuff in here." Adrian held out his hand.

Dalton ignored the handshake offer. He probably couldn't even see Adrian's hand. His emerald-green eyes were locked on mine with an intensity I had never seen in person. I knew the look, though. It was the expression Sir Drake Cheshire, his supernatural character on *One Vamp to Love*, got right before he bit someone. Not in the sexy way, either.

Adrian said, "We were doing the scene where David and Harper—"

"Leave," Dalton commanded, his whole body radiating fury.

Adrian lifted his chin defiantly and didn't budge. "I have a right to be here."

"He's my friend," I said.

Dalton's eyes continued blazing at me. "What's that on your shirt?"

I looked down. "Ketchup," I said. I'd forgotten about the ketchup. Not only was it smeared down the front of my shirt but it was all over Adrian's shirt. Talk about being busted red-handed, or red-chested. Literally.

"So," Dalton said, speaking slowly. "You are two old friends who were doing a scene from my movie?"

"Basically," I said.

He didn't budge. I was dimly aware that the music had stopped in the other room, and that people were watching from the other side of the doorway. Great. Now we had an audience for our little melodrama.

Dalton's emerald-green eyes narrowed. "How did you get that script?"

"Your butler gave it to me by accident," I said coolly. "Which reminds me, I need to get a copy of that NDA I signed. You can have your people send it by email to my dad."

A moment of tense silence passed.

Then Adrian said, "I have a few questions about this script." He'd been leafing through it as we stood there. "I haven't read the whole thing or seen a treatment, but you're the expert, so I'll ask you. Is this a film about a famous guy who romances a two-dimensional chubby girl in his old hometown?"

Dalton flicked his eyes over to Adrian, which was a relief for me, but I did start worrying about Adrian's safety. I knew Dalton didn't have actual vampire teeth for biting people, yet some part of me wasn't so sure about that. I'd seen him bite a lot of people. On TV, but still.

The handsome yet angry actor replied tersely, "Harper is a three-dimensional character."

"Sure she is," Adrian said, wearing the smug, know-it-all grin he wore so well. "She's a three-dimensional character who exists only as a foil to Mr. Perfect, David, who is God's gift to humanity. This guy is over the top. I mean, he's a poet, a singer, the owner of a tech company, and a humanitarian. Harper's main tag is that she jiggles and giggles. It's pretty obvious that her role in this story is to serve as the conduit for Mr. Perfect's character arc change, which is what? Realizing that there's nothing wrong with him?"

Dalton's expression faltered. "Who are you again?"

"Adrian Stromquist." Adrian offered his hand again. "I've been doing real estate the past few years, but I am available as a script doctor. Or, if you're looking for a new project, I have a few ideas I can pitch you."

Dalton said, "You're a writer, when you're not kissing my..." He looked at me. His lips moved as he struggled to find the right word without the help of a script. "Peaches," he said, finishing the thought.

I was relieved. I'd thought for sure he was going to call me by the name of my doppelganger character in the script, Harper.

Adrian pulled his rejected hand back for a second time and chuckled. "That's right," he said. "I'm a script doctor and writer when I'm not kissing your Peaches."

Dalton said nothing. He kept his lips shut, concealing any actual vampire teeth that might have been emerging.

Adrian turned to me and said, "Well, it's getting late. I should get home to take Cujo for his run. Maybe I'll see you later, if you're out in the woods." He turned to Dalton and said, "Good to meet you, Mr. Deangelo. Sorry about the awkward timing. See you around, man." He started toward the back door but paused. "Take good care of our Peaches. She talks tough, but she bruises easily."

Then he left.

Dalton and I weren't exactly alone in the kitchen.

My best friend and a crowd of our old high school friends were watching from the other doorway.

I looked down at the ketchup on my shirt. Considering I'd smeared it on Adrian while we were kissing, there was still a lot of ketchup there. I picked up my second sausage roll, dipped it in the chest ketchup, then ate it.

Dalton turned to the crowd behind him and said, "Aren't you supposed to be having a party?"

Nisha apologized and herded everyone away from the door. The music came back on in the other room.

Dalton crossed the kitchen to where Adrian had set the script. He picked it up like it weighed a hundred pounds.

"This is an older version," he said. "We've made extensive changes."

"Oh?" I batted my eyelashes at him. "Is Harper still fat and two-dimensional? The regular-girl foil to your Mr. Perfect?"

"The actress playing Harper brings a lot of depth that isn't on the page," he said.

"But does she jiggle and giggle?"

He turned his head slowly. "Are you upset with me?"

"That depends," I said. "What am I to you? Tell me the truth. Am I your research?"

"What if you are my research? Does it matter?"

His callous words were a slap in the face. Did it matter? Did it matter if I was research?

The room was spinning and blurry. I was too upset to see straight. I turned around and started tidying up the counter.

"Just go," I said, not looking at Dalton. "You got your research. You found out what it feels like to break the heart of a regular girl who's not perfect like you. What more do you want from me?"

Softly, he said, "Peaches."

"Don't call me that. My name is Petra. That other name is what my friends call me." I kept my gaze on the blurry pile of party debris in front of me. "As far as I'm concerned, you and I are not friends. We were only business colleagues. I helped you with your movie research, and now we're done."

"You can't say that."

I whirled around to face him. I couldn't tell what my face was doing, but whatever it was, it made Dalton take two steps back in shock.

"I'm not Harper," I said. "I haven't been pining away for you my whole life. I didn't even start watching your show until it was three seasons in, and I didn't even like it that much. It happened to be on at a time that worked for my schedule. My whole life doesn't revolve around you, *David*. I mean Dalton. So why don't you take your stupid little script for your stupid little movie, and go find someone else to run lines with? I'm sure there are lots of girls around who'd be happy to"—I made air quotes with my fingers—"*kiss you like you're dangerous.*"

He shook the script at me. "Tell me again. How did you get this?"

"Bernard gave it to me. He was supposed to give me a copy of the contract I signed, but he must have given that to me by mistake."

Dalton stepped back slowly. "Bernard doesn't make mistakes," he said.

"Good for him," I said. "I make plenty of mistakes, and you were one of them."

"Don't say that."

"Too late. We're way off the script now, pretty boy."

He blinked at me, stunned.

"Now leave," I said. "Please leave so I can enjoy the rest of my five-year high school reunion."

Dalton looked down at the script then up at me. He looked confused. Lost. He was breathing rapidly, his breath high in his chest.

With a choked-sounding voice, he said, "I need some air."

I went to the back door and yanked it open. "Take all the air you need."

Then he left.

He didn't come back.

I walked out to the living room, where everyone pretended they hadn't been listening in to the entire thing.

Someone handed me a drink, and we got the party going again.

I focused on the positive: Nisha had quit her job and was free to pursue other adventures.

That was enough for a celebration. That was enough to keep me from crying. Plus there was plenty of booze. It's a scientific fact that you can't sob while drinking; you'll choke and die if you do.

The party did pick up again. Sunshine Banks hauled me onto our makeshift stage for a karaoke duet, and I killed.

Dalton Deangelo didn't return to the house party that night.

I didn't hear from him the next day, either.

On Monday, I became curious enough to phone him—I was planning to hang up as soon as he answered—only to find that the number had been discontinued.

Time passed. My broken heart crusted over.

Two weeks after the house party and presumed breakup, I packed my bags and flew to LA for my modeling contract.

Dalton and I were over, and the press knew—he'd issued a brief statement—but the publicity team at the studio still wanted me for my modeling contract. They wanted me more than ever. By rejecting Mr. Perfect, I had increased my value. Who knew?

It was too bad I didn't feel that way about myself.

Perhaps meditation would help. Or something more tangible.

Chapter 2

The photos had been taken. No more sitting in the makeup chair. No more getting fitted in underwear by a team of chilly-fingered photographer assistants. I was done until the next season.

Friday afternoon, I boarded the plane to head home.

I was wearing the same peach-colored warm-up suit I'd worn on the flight in, yet I felt like a completely new Peaches. My old, regular life had involved getting a mocha at Donut Joe's then talking about books all day. For the last week, I'd spent my days meditating in the makeup chair and then being told how gorgeous I was while a photographer snapped away.

My week in Los Angeles had been intense and uplifting. I'd made friends with some other models, including a very appealing young man who was well-known for his calendars. We'd gotten extra friendly. But my favorite person was Mitchell, the brand manager who was in charge of the entire campaign.

Mitchell was a compact guy with a flair for fashion, if you know what I mean. He was better at fashion than anyone I'd ever met. He was also a gay man. Not that those two things were always connected, but in Mitchell's case, they were.

I settled into my seat on the airplane and sent Mitchell one last text thanking him for taking me under his wing. I told him I'd miss him, and it wasn't just fake LA show business talk. I really would miss him.

He texted back that he missed me already and was crying into a peach milkshake. He had dropped me off at the airport two hours earlier, and had solemnly pledged to break his diet to properly mourn my leaving town.

After I shut off my phone and put it away, the elderly gentleman seated next to me on the flight turned to me and said, "Now, there's no need to be nervous about flying, young lady."

"I know," I said. "I've heard the statistics. Flying is safer than crossing the street."

My seatmate nodded, a twinkle in his eye as he pointed up with one finger. "Plus, in all of aviation history, they've never left one single person up there."

I gave him the laugh he wanted. "That's a good one. I'll have to tell my dad."

His eyes still twinkling, the man asked, "Are you a movie star?"

I laughed again and flicked my blond locks over my shoulder. "Just a model," I said. "A *different* kind of model, obviously."

"Good for you," he said. "You give 'em heck."

"I will."

He pulled out his paperback novel—the new spy thriller that Bernard and the rest of the world had been anticipating—and began reading.

I settled into my seat and nodded off.

As we flew away from California, I dreamed that Mitchell and I, plus a group of attractive underwear models, had trespassed our way into a fancy swimming pool in the Hollywood Hills. We'd had quite the adventure in my dream. The reality was, I'd barely had a moment to take a dip in the hotel pool, let alone traipse all over LA with a model posse.

When I woke up, my seatmate was fast asleep—not dead—I checked—and we were landing already.

I could see why my home city was so popular as an alternative filming location. The direct flight from LA was a breeze. I'd spent more time in makeup stores, trying on lipstick.

With my carry-on bag trailing behind me on its wheels, I walked into Arrivals, where my father had promised to meet me to drive me home. He wasn't there. Not alone, anyway.

My mother, my father, and Elliot were all there, holding one of those signs that drivers held up with the names of people they were picking up. The Monroes—*my* Monroes—were holding a comically large sign that read: PEACHES MONROE, SUPERMODEL.

To say I got a little emotional would be an understatement.

There's nothing like being away for a week to make you appreciate home and the people who love you.

Chapter 3

Saturday, June 11th

The regular customers at Bookworm Books were not impressed by my recent week-long adventure as a underwear model.

All day at work, I had to answer the same questions about where I'd been, and why some woman named Rhonda had been in the store when I should have been there. I was glad Rhonda wasn't around to hear them complain about her. So what if she didn't know as much about books as I did? At least the store had been open. To hear people moan about it, you'd think I'd put a padlock on the door and abandoned the place.

When my coworker, Garnet Langtree, came in to work his afternoon shift, I thought I'd get a break from all the attitude. No break was given. Garnet was in a mood about something.

We got a moment alone, and I said to the sixteen-year-old, "I know the employee manual forbids corporal punishment, but I am your manager, and I will double-punch you in the butt if you keep giving me those dirty looks."

Garnet unpacked a box of paperbacks furiously.

"Hey," I said. "I'm talking to you."

The dark-haired teen flattened the empty box with fiery vengeance.

"You get paid to be here, kiddo," I said. "Help like this, I don't need."

He scowled.

I asked, "What's going on with you?"

It all came out in a burst. "Why did you have to break up with him?" He directed his angry energy at me, eyes blazing.

"Are you referring to Dalton Deangelo?"

"Duh."

I resisted the urge to strangle him. "First of all, I did not break up with him, because we were never really together. Second of all, it was three weeks ago, which makes the whole thing ancient news. Thirdly, since when is my romantic life any of your business?"

"Since my mom cancelled her trip home so she could go visit that loser in rehab."

"What?" I stared at him.

He returned my stare with a side of *duh*. "You don't know?"

"Dalton's in rehab? I have no idea what you're talking about. Did something happen this week? I was pretty busy running around in my underwear and getting paid about a hundred times what I make here."

"It was the week before last. My mom says she's only there to support him *as a friend*, but I've heard that one before."

"He's in rehab? Are you sure? Where did you hear that?"

"From her," he said, his eyes wide with passive aggression. "From Jade."

Garnet's mother was Jade, the famous pop singer whose sexy poster had been on every teen boy's bedroom wall when I had been his age.

"Does everyone know?"

Garnet said, "The press doesn't know." His attitude softened as he realized I was unaware of the developments he was talking about. "It's not a rehab for drugs specifically. My mother said he's there for anxiety. It's one of those fancy places in Malibu. They've got horses and alpacas."

"I love alpacas."

"Who doesn't? It's the fuzzy eyelashes."

"Are you saying Dalton's in LA? But I was just there," I said with disbelief. "I didn't see him."

Garnet stared at me like I was an idiot. "It's a big city, Peaches."

"I mean I didn't see him at the photo shoots. A bunch of his other costars were there, because of the cross-promo branding thing." I rubbed my chin. "Come to think about it, they were all pretty hush-hush about why Dalton wouldn't be dropping by. I assumed it was because of me. Was it actually about rehab?"

Garnet shrugged. "I guess so."

"What about *Waterfall*? The movie he was shooting here?"

"They had to shut down production. It's going to cost the studio a fortune."

"Maybe it's for the best," I said. "That movie looked like a dud. I wish I'd kept the script. You would have laughed so hard."

Garnet's shoulders slumped. He relaxed and sat on the edge of the table we'd been using for unpacking stock.

"Sorry I got mad at you," he said. "It's not your fault. My mom is the one who comes up with any excuse not to come home and see her family."

"Oh, kiddo." I came over to where he was sitting and gave him a big hug. Garnet was nine years older than the boy I'd given birth to, but sometimes my motherly feelings came out. The strangling and the hugging. Mothers don't get to pick and choose.

Garnet called his mother a bad word.

I reflexively came to her defense, as moms sometimes do. "Being a mother is hard. Take it easy on her, and remember you've always got me."

He groaned about being hugged but didn't try to escape.

I let him go once he stopped hating the hug and started melting into it.

"Thanks," he said, shrugging, tossing his hair, and generally trying to regain his cool after having been hugged.

We resumed unpacking the boxes.

A funny thought occurred to me, so I shared it with the teenager.

"Nisha thinks Dalton Deangelo owes you an apology," I said. "I had a crazy idea, and I talked to her about it, since she's the expert on all that karma stuff. She agrees that your connection is probably why he came running in here that day. If you hadn't been late for work that Saturday, you might have gotten the apology he owes you. Then I wouldn't have fallen into his arms, and then everything would have been different."

Rather than tell me I was crazy, Garnet said, "I'm sorry I slept in that day."

"And I'm sorry you didn't get your karma apology from the man who busted up your family. What a guy."

"He didn't bust up anything that wasn't already broken," Garnet said.

"Sure, but he didn't help, either."

"I hate famous people," Garnet said. "Remind me to never get famous."

"Will you hate me when I become famous for modeling underwear?"

He wrinkled his nose.

"It could happen," I said. "I may have the X factor. It's been over three weeks now since my hot springs pictures, and the internet hasn't forgotten about me yet. Not completely."

"You're not as popular as the girl with the bees."

"No, but you don't know her name. People know my name. I'm Peaches by the Pound."

"Yeah, yeah," he said dismissively. "It's four o'clock. You can go now."

"Oh, can I?" I ruffled his dark hair on the way out. "Hang in there," I said. "Your mother will get her priorities right eventually. Keep your chin up, kiddo. It's always darkest before the dawn."

"No, it's not. It's light for an hour before dawn. It's called *the blue hour*."

"You are too smart for this place. Get a better college degree than mine so you can get a job where your talents aren't wasted."

"You know my family's rich, right? I don't need to work."

I pointed at him as I pushed open the front door to leave. "I do know. You're exactly the sort of person we look for to work in a bookstore."

I stepped outside into the June heat. It wasn't California, but the city was warming up.

As I walked home, I mulled over the news Garnet had given me.

According to him, and his direct connection via Jade, Dalton Deangelo had walked off his movie project and checked into a treatment center for anxiety. I wondered if it had anything to do with me.

I immediately laughed off the idea. There was no way.

He and I had been involved, sort of, for just short of two weeks. As of that Saturday, it had been three weeks since I'd seen him—a week longer than we'd been together. Nobody checked into rehab for a two-week relationship. Especially not one that had been more about movie role research than romance.

Then again, he had looked anxious and upset when he'd left my house that Friday night, saying he needed air.

But on the other hand, Adrian had just told him how terrible his movie was. Adrian Stromquist had superpowers when it came to making people feel stupid. When he found out I hadn't realized I was pregnant until I was giving birth, the looks Adrian had given me were worse than the labor pains.

Okay, that was an exaggeration. Nothing was worse than labor pains.

But Adrian's smug derision could really sting.

What must have happened that night was that Dalton realized he was in a stinker of a movie and figured his only way out was to stage a fake meltdown.

That had to be it.

Chapter 4

To celebrate my triumphant and safe return home from my first modeling gig, Nisha offered to take me out for dinner and drinks at O'Flannigan's. Or, as she liked to call the place, O'Hannigan's. The lettering on the sign for the pub had confusing serifs, where the F-L looked a lot like an H, which led to many drunken debates inside the pub about what the place was called. The same lettering was on the menus and beer coasters, which didn't help settle anything.

I headed to the pub as soon as I left Bookworm Books.

The party was well underway by the time dinner time came around. Then dinner time passed, and we forgot to order dinner. The nacho platter had been enough to mildly interfere with our alcohol consumption.

It was a party of four giggling girls. The Quad Squad. Two of our former high school friends that we'd recently connected with, Brittany Brown and Sunshine Banks, joined us.

Brittany was small, blond, and perky. Her signature move was kicking up one foot behind her when she got excited. Sunshine was tall, dark, and sultry. Sunshine dreamed of stardom as a singer, and never missed an opportunity to show off the butterfly tattoos on her lower back.

Earlier that summer, Brittany had been dating Nisha's former boss, Noah. Both of them were over him now. The two of them had been bonding heavily over what a jerk he was. They entertained us for over an hour with stories about how lousy the guy was in bed. Nisha had only been with him once, but she had an excellent memory for detail. Plus she'd been pining after the man for years, so she'd been primed to compare every second of reality to all her fantasies.

I didn't speak up about it, but it reminded me of my one night of passion with Dalton Deangelo, when we'd threatened to rock his Airstream trailer off its supports. Unlike Nisha's time with Noah, that night had not been a disappointment. I'd fantasized plenty about being with Dalton, or at least with his vampire character, and I'd seen countless love scenes on the soapy drama. The reality of being with him had far surpassed everything in my imagination.

I was sick of the guy now, and I'd never watch him on TV or in a movie ever again, but I'd always have that perfect night in my memory, and that was something. Now that my crusty old broken heart had healed, I was starting to feel different about my experience with the actor. The bad ending had dulled, and only the good parts remained. We'd had some nice times together, joking about meatballs at Niro's. Plus the hot spring had been magical.

My mind kept straying back to my time with Dalton, so I drank faster to fuzz it out.

The three girls at my table were more than entertaining enough, anyway. It felt good to be with friends, just laughing like idiots, the way we used to back in high school.

There came a relatively quiet moment when we weren't acting hysterical. Sunshine turned to me and said, "I've been to Jade's house."

The other two fell silent and stared at me. Brittany's gaze was unfocused. The tiny blonde was swaying like she was at sea. Nisha wasn't as inebriated, but she was blinking way more than usual.

I gave Sunshine a nonverbal, flat response about Jade. It wouldn't be enough to get her to back off.

Sunshine had been digging so hard for dirt about me and Dalton that I wondered if she wasn't working undercover as a reporter.

"Jade's got a really nice house," Sunshine said. "My brother was friends with Jade's daughter for a while. Now she's dating my ex, Marcus. The daughter, not Jade. Her name's Perry."

"I know all about that whole thing from last summer," I said. "I work with Garnet, remember?"

"Garnet's a sweet kid," Sunshine said. "I saw him the other day at the bookstore. He's growing up fast, and he's not bad looking." She chewed on the cherry from her drink suggestively. "He might be ready to date in a few years."

All three of us turned on Sunshine and booed her. Brittany didn't know what we were booing about, but she was a team booer.

"Easy, girls," Sunshine said. "It was just a joke. I'm not like that anymore. I know I'll make it on my own someday, and I don't need to get favors from anyone." She turned to me and batted her long, dark eyelashes. "But if your underwear people happen to need a diverse model in my color for a new campaign, I am available."

"I'll keep it in mind," I said. Sunshine claimed to be a changed person who wasn't all about stardom, but she hadn't changed since high school. She wasn't a terrible human being—we wouldn't have been friends with her if she was—but her career aspirations did cloud her judgement when it came to using people. As a person who'd recently been used as a research project by a certain well-known TV vampire, I was particularly sensitive to such a thing.

Sunshine fixed her dark-brown eyes on me. "So? What really happened after you kicked your boy Dalton out of the house?"

"You were there," I said. "All of you were there. After he left, I proceeded to drink way too many paralyzers, or White Russians, or whatever those drinks were."

"It was mudslides," Nisha said.

"Ooh," Brittany said, smacking her lips. "Mudslides are *amazeballs*."

"Mudslides," I agreed. "That was it. And, as for what happened between me and Dalton, there's nothing more to tell. I haven't even talked to the guy since that night."

"That's odd," Sunshine said. "Not even a few text messages?"

"He's busy," I said. I did not tell her I'd phoned and discovered his number had been changed. "Whatever. It's over."

Sunshine held her hand to her chest. "To me, it did not sound like it was over. What do you guys think?"

She and I looked over at the other two.

Nisha said, "It's not over. You two are way too tangled up in each other." She made a gesture with her hands, interlocking her fingers.

Brittany, who was barely holding onto the conversation thread, said, "I like Drake. He's a good vampire."

I gave Nisha a dirty look. "It's over. You cleansed my aura, and I started meditating, and I received a message from the cosmos that it's over." I tapped my temple. "A voice told me."

Nisha shook her head and said to Sunshine, "Peaches thinks that sitting for fifteen minutes without looking at her phone is the same thing as meditating."

Sunshine frowned. "It's not?"

"Not at all," Nisha said.

Brittany said, "Hello, phone," and stared blankly at the back of her phone. "Turn on," she said, poking the plastic case.

Nisha said to Sunshine, "People with lower blood volume can't handle as much alcohol as us big girls."

Sunshine snorted. "Who are you calling a big girl?"

"You're tall," Nisha said. "You weigh as much as I do."

"No," Sunshine said. "No way. I'm not a *big* girl." She glanced my way.

I was not enjoying the direction the conversation was going.

Just then, my bladder gave me a signal I couldn't ignore. I got up from my chair.

"Don't do it," Brittany said to me, dropping her phone. "Don't break the seal."

"Yeah," Sunshine said to me. "Don't break the seal. Once you start going to the washroom, you'll be going all night."

I patted her on the shoulder on my way by. "Better than having to go in the alley or on someone's lawn after we walk out of here, like I'm sure you three dummies will be doing tonight."

The three of them went, "OooOOOoooh!"

I made my way over to the ladies' room, where I freshened up.

On my way back to the table, a tall man with blond hair blocked my path.

"I'm not your serving wench, buddy," I said, darting around him.

"Peaches!"

I turned around quickly, nearly falling over. I shouldn't have had so many adult beverages and zero dinner.

"Stormy Weather Adrian," I said.

He reached out to steady me, then gave me a concerned look. "Are you okay? I haven't seen you since your party. My mom said that your mom told her you went to Los Angeles and did a photo shoot in your underwear. Is it true?"

To answer him, I did what seemed easier than using words. Keep in mind I was quite inebriated.

I lifted my shirt and said, "Get a load of these!"

I was wearing a bra from the line I'd been modeling. I was now a spokesmodel, so I had plenty of fancy underwear to choose from. Every day was a fancy underwear day now.

Adrian quickly yanked the shirt back down and glanced around, embarrassed. "You're drunk," he said.

"That's what we do at O'Flannigan's," I said. "Why are you here? Shouldn't you be working on your new screenplays?"

"I am working." He gestured to a small table at the edge of the pub where a laptop was sitting open. "I figured I'd get out of the house for some inspiration."

I stared up at him. He was so pretty. Not like how girls were pretty, but like how some boys were pretty. I could stare at him all night long.

He snapped his fingers in front of my face. "Are you okay?"

I threw my arms in the air. "Take me drunk! I'm home!"

"You do need to go home," he said. "Who are you here with?"

"The cheerleaders," I said. It was true. All three of the girls I'd been drinking with had been cheerleaders in high school.

Adrian grabbed my hand, dragged me over to his table, made me hold his laptop while he pulled on his jacket, then dragged me over to my friends. He informed them that it was time for everyone to call it a night.

All three of them refused, so he negotiated for my solo release and then dragged me away. It all happened rather quickly.

Suddenly, we were outside, on the sidewalk in front of O'Flannigan's.

My ears were ringing from the music and noise of the pub, plus the effects of the alcohol.

I looked up at Adrian and said, "What?"

"I didn't say anything," he said. "It's only about ten blocks to your house, right?"

"Which one? The house that I pay for with my boob money or the one that my mom paid for with her sex money?"

Adrian scrunched up his face in confusion. "What?"

"Oh. You don't know! It's a long story, and I can't tell you because you would put it in your movie and then you would make me do research with you," I rambled drunkenly. "I want to do research with you, Adrian, but you are bad for me and you always get me in trouble. I wish you weren't so pretty."

He tried to take his laptop back from me, but I fought him—for absolutely no reason except I didn't want to give in to him in any way whatsoever.

"Fine," he said. "Carry my laptop all the way to your place. But if you drop it or throw up on it, I'm going to make you pay for another one."

"I'll take it out of your child support that you don't pay."

He stopped and put one hand over my mouth. "Shh," he said. "Maybe don't talk for a while."

I responded by licking his hand. Then I sucked on his fingers. He pulled his hand away and gave me a look I hadn't seen on his face in a long time. Not since those nights back at his house, when we'd been working on ideas for romance scenes in our screenplay.

He wiped his hand on his jeans, grabbed me by the hand, and started walking us toward my house.

We'd made it about two blocks when he stopped suddenly.

"Peaches," he said. "What was that noise?"

I poked him on the nose with one finger. "It's just the sound of you, throwing yourself at my feet, big boy."

"Not now. I hear something."

"It might be the paparazzi sneaking up to take pictures of me. It's a good thing I look so great." I was wearing a basic pair of jeans with a T-shirt, but I felt great. It had to be the fancy underwear I had on under my regular clothes.

He gave me a sidelong look. "You do look amazing. I'll admit that much." His eyes roved up and down over my body. "Your body just doesn't quit. Can you please stop being so sexy around me? I can't stop looking."

I blinked up at him. "Why would you ever want to stop?"

Something made a noise. I heard it that time.

I called out to the darkness, "Josie Ranger? Is that you? Are you here to get your freckles punched off?" I tried to punch my fist into my palm and nearly dropped Adrian's laptop.

Chapter 5

I called her name again, but Josie Ranger didn't step out of the shadows.

Adrian asked me, "Who's that?"

"Nobody you'd know," I said, waving one hand just enough to nearly tip myself over in my inebriated state.

"I know that name. Are you talking about Jocko Ranger's daughter? I've seen her around lately. Do you know her?"

"Never mind about any of Jocko Ranger's kids." I poked him on the nose again. "Boop."

Something shadowy came out from behind a hedge. Another shadow followed it. The shadows were larger than cats.

"Oh, it's just raccoons," Adrian said.

I jumped back. "What do you mean, *just raccoons*? They're aggressive in this neighborhood. They're city raccoons, Adrian. They will mug you."

"Don't be silly." Adrian called out to the raccoons, "C'mere, little guys. Come say hi."

I turned and watched in horror as one raccoon ambled toward us, followed by two more.

My reflexes were slow from drinking, but I sure as heck wasn't sticking around to get mauled by raccoons.

I resumed walking toward my house, faster than ever.

Adrian laughed at me as he easily caught up on his long legs.

Several blocks of speed-walking away from city raccoons in the fresh night air worked wonders on my inebriation levels.

By the time we reached my house, I was able to walk in a straight line. Almost.

"Come inside," I said. "We have lots of ketchup. I'll make you sausage rolls."

He held back. "I shouldn't."

"Sausage rolls," I said, as enticingly as I could. "You know you want some," I growled.

"You shouldn't be using a hot oven in this state," he said, and he followed me inside.

It was going to take the oven thirty minutes to heat the sausage rolls from their frozen state. I tried to microwave them, but Adrian wouldn't let me.

During the very long wait for the oven, Adrian managed to keep me away from the alcohol cupboard while also getting some water into me.

Soon, I was feeling just sober enough to feel embarrassed by my actions, but not sober enough to stop myself.

Adrian pulled the sausage rolls from the oven. He kept me away while they cooled by using the tongs to pinch me if I tried to get one.

Finally, we hunkered down over the kitchen table and ate the sausage rolls dipped in ketchup.

They were good. It had been worth the wait to toast them properly in the oven. Microwaved pastry was for people who, deep down, hated themselves.

I was just sober enough to not get ketchup on my shirt. I was not sober enough to stop myself from pulling down the neck of my shirt, placing a sausage roll in my cleavage, and saying, "Come and get it, big boy. Dinner is served."

Adrian's expression cracked for the first time that evening. He'd been so stern and judgemental, a younger version of his father, Erik Stromquist. But while looking at the sausage roll in my cleavage, he changed back to the Adrian I'd fallen for back in high school. The Adrian who could be moody and broody, but also fun and full of excitement.

"That's the last one," Adrian said, licking his lips. "It would be a shame to waste it."

"Exactly," I said. "You get the picture."

"I know what's happening here," he said, leaning back. "I'm not falling into your trap, even though it's a very appealing trap."

"What trap?"

"Your boob trap," he said. "You want to use me like a drug, to change how you feel."

"I do not."

"You're upset about that actor jerk. You want someone to fill the void and get you high again."

"Have you been talking to Nisha?"

"We hung out a bit when you were in LA."

"Nisha overthinks everything. You can't take life advice from her."

"Who should I take life advice from?"

"From your own experiences." I looked down. "That sausage roll looks so good. It would be a shame if nobody ate it."

"You want me to eat that sausage roll, don't you?"

"I want you to try." I grinned. "I double dare you to try."

He moved his chair closer to mine.

I moved my chair away.

He raised an eyebrow. "Is this how it's going to be? You want me to chase you?"

"This is how it always goes," I said. "I never threw myself at you, Adrian. You were always chasing me. It was always you."

He slid toward me.

I slid back.

He eyed the sausage roll, licked his lips, and slid forward quickly.

I jumped off my chair and started running.

He was after me, right on my heels.

I didn't know where I was going, and there wasn't far to go in the small house. He chased me through the living room, down the hallway, and into Nisha's room. He stood at the doorway with his arms outstretched, grinning at having trapped me.

I double-punched him in the solar plexus then shimmied past him.

Groaning and moaning about having been hit, he continued his pursuit. We circled through the living room again, through the kitchen, out the back door, around the side of the house, in the front door, through the living room, and then—you already know where this is going—into my bedroom.

I was breathing heavily as I backed up toward my bed.

He dropped his shoulders and made his body wide as he advanced toward me, as serious as a spy in an action movie trying to get the secret codes from an enemy spy.

He came at me in a blur of speed.

It wasn't until he had his face buried in my chest that I remembered I'd put a sausage roll there.

He pulled back, grinning and triumphant.

I waited until he'd chewed the sausage roll before I threw myself at him.

He fell back on my bed with no resistance.

I was on top of him, and our noses were nearly touching.

Adrian said, "You don't even want me. You just want a warm body to soften your fall."

"Oh, shush. Why can't we enjoy being two warm bodies?"

He frowned. "I don't know. Why can't we?"

I was about to kiss him when I felt a warning tremor in my stomach. I held back, incredibly confused by two conflicting feelings. On the one hand, there was the intense sensation of lust that I felt in every cell of my body, some areas more than others. On the other hand, I might throw up at any moment.

Adrian stared up at me, his beautiful angular features looking so gorgeous in the dim streetlamp light coming in through my window.

"I missed you, Peaches," he said. "I've really missed this. I've missed us."

He reached up and swept some of my hair away from my face.

The queasiness remained, along with the lust. I didn't dare move.

A line from the script came to me. "You wouldn't have to miss me so much if you hadn't left me here," I said.

He frowned. "Is that a line from *Waterfall*?"

"I may be paraphrasing."

He wriggled upward on the bed and propped himself up on his elbows. "Are you running lines on me?"

"So what if I am?" I rolled back into a seating position. "It's what all the cool kids are doing." My stomach made a noise. Not a pleasant one.

He squirmed away from me and jumped off the bed like it was covered in an unpleasant substance.

"Let's, uh, get you some more water," he said.

"No need," I said, getting up and pushing my way past him. "It'll just be more stuff for me to have to throw up."

I went to the washroom and closed the door behind me. I wasn't sick yet, but I would be.

He tapped on the door. "Do you want me to stay?"

"You can go," I said. "Nisha will be home eventually."

"Are you sure?"

"Just go," I said, a little louder. He was starting to annoy me. Or my stomach was annoyed. It was hard to tell the difference.

"I'm not leaving," he said. "I'll be in the living room until someone else gets here to take care of you."

I yelled at the door, "I can take care of myself!"

It was, ironically, exactly the sort of thing someone who's not doing a good job taking care of herself will scream at people.

The other side of the door went quiet.

I leaned over the toilet, and, well, you can guess the rest.

Chapter 6

The following morning, my brain featured a double matinée showing of that movie nobody wants to see:*Embarrassing Highlights From Last Night*.

Let's call this film EHLN for short.

With a groan, I crawled out of bed while EHLN continued to play in my head.

As I was brushing the fuzz out of my mouth, the film reached the point where Adrian and I were in the kitchen, and I'd just put a sausage roll in my cleavage. Had that actually happened? I looked down at myself. I had pastry crumbs all down the center of my chest. It must have happened.

What else? Oh, Adrian had accused me of setting up a trap. A boob trap. Then he'd said, "You want to use me like a drug, to change how you feel."

I had denied it, of course.

Then he'd accused me of being upset about Dalton, and acting out because of it. He'd said, "You want someone to fill the void and get you high again."

I brushed my teeth hard, trying to get EHLN to stop playing. The film reached the part where I'd thrown Adrian onto my bed and had been about to kiss him.

Adrian had said, "You don't even want me. You just want a warm body to soften your fall."

As much as it hurt, I had to admit to myself—in the stark light of morning—that he hadn't been wrong. I hadn't been thinking about Adrian's feelings, or his life, or what it might mean to him if I'd kissed him.

Nisha had mentioned something about a romance blossoming between him and Brittany Brown. Had I ruined Adrian's chance at happiness with Brittany by leaving the pub with him last night? If Brittany was interested in him, it must have broken her heart to see us walk out together.

The film playing on repeat in my head taught me a valuable lesson: I was a lousy person who used other people.

There was something wrong with me. I needed to stop hurting people, and stop being such a mess.

And I would.

But first, pancakes.

I went to Nisha's room and peeked in. She had made it home from the pub safely, along with both Brittany and Sunshine. They had crashed on Nisha's bed on either side of her. Nisha had a king-sized bed —it had been a hand-me-down from a family member—so there was plenty of room. The three girls looked cute together, with their blond hair, straight black hair, and curly black hair with highlights mingling together on the pillows.

I left them to sleep off their fun night out and went to the kitchen.

I smelled coffee before I'd even walked in. Adrian was in the kitchen, shirtless. He was relaxing at the kitchen table with a cup of coffee.

"You spent the night," I said.

"It looks that way." He gave me his annoying know-it-all grin. His long, angular features were particularly sharp and mocking that morning.

"You'd better put a shirt on before I attack you," I said. "You know how I am around warm male bodies. I want them, like a drug. Or was it a mattress to fall on? I can't remember which metaphor you stuck with."

He gave me a blank stare.

I remembered the resolution I'd made in the bathroom to not be such a lousy person. Oops. Resolutions never last very long.

"Just joking," I said.

"Right," he said. "Listen, if I said anything last night that bothered you, I didn't mean it."

"Why would you say it if you didn't mean it?"

He grabbed his shirt and pulled it on, which was probably for the best. The sight of his tanned, chiseled abdomen, with its thin line of golden curls, was having an effect on me. I was, after all, only human.

Patiently, he said, "What I mean is, I didn't say any of that stuff to hurt you. I'm just, you know, trying to get to the truth underneath everything."

I poured myself some coffee and joined him. "The truth underneath everything," I said. "I remember that. Do you still have that tattoo?" Adrian had gotten a Japanese kanji character tattooed on his ankle back in high school. He'd used his older cousin Lars Lundin's ID to get it.

He looked away. "Yeah. Tattoos are permanent."

The kanji character was in the form of a person who was upside down, which indicated that the person was dead. The truth was that all of us would die someday. The whole thing had appealed to the moody, brooding aspect of the guy I called Stormy Weather Adrian.

"They're not *that* permanent," I said. "You can get them lasered off."

"Maybe I like having it there," he said. "It reminds me of the ideals I used to have."

I sipped my coffee. "What do you mean, the ideals you used to have? Are you a heartless, soulless sellout now? Did real estate make you that phony?"

He gave me a defeated look. "It might have. I'm not getting anywhere with my screenplay."

"That's because you never could write on your own," I said.

He frowned. "I could, too. And I might have gotten a chance to, if you'd ever left me alone."

"Let's face it," I said. "We worked better as a team. Neither of us could write on our own, but that screenplay we turned in was box office gold."

"It was," he said. "I regret deleting the document when... everything happened."

"When everything happened? You mean when *your progeny* came screaming out of my uterus?"

He looked away. "Don't say it like that. Why do you have to phrase things in the worst possible way?"

"I'm direct."

"You could be less direct."

"Why?"

He shook his head.

"Gotcha," I said. "Two points for Peaches."

"About last night," he said slowly.

"What about it?"

There was a knock at the front door.

I gave Adrian a confused look. "Who could that be? Everyone I know is here inside this house right now."

I went to see who was banging on my door on a Sunday at the crack of noon.

Chapter 7

I would never admit it out loud, but deep down I hoped that the person knocking on my door at the crack of noon that Sunday was Dalton Deangelo.

I opened the door to find a different handsome—yet much older—man standing on the porch.

Gordon Olivier. My boss and the owner of Bookworm Books, along with several other storefronts on Baker Street.

"Mr. Olivier," I said excitedly. "You're back from Arizona!"

"It is June, *ma chérie*," he said in his charming French accent. "I do not like frying eggs on the hood of my car, and I do not like Arizona in the summer."

"That sounds like a page from a children's book. You just need a little green ham in there." I waved for him to come inside. "What can I do for you today?" The bookstore was closed most Sundays, so I knew I wasn't in trouble for not showing up at work.

He stepped in and removed his hat. Gordon always wore a fedora, no matter the weather.

"Forgive me for intruding on your private time, but I wanted to speak with you about a business matter."

His serious tone caused my heart to sink. "You're not shutting it down, are you? I know sales aren't the best, but I've got some ideas for saving money."

"Tut-tut," he said, and waved his hand. "Do not be alarmed. I am making changes, but it is in the interest of preserving the bookstore."

"That's a relief," I said with a sigh. "My career as an underwear model hasn't taken off yet."

He looked over my shoulder. Adrian had entered the living room.

Gordon said, "Forgive me for interrupting your time together." He offered his hand to Adrian. "Gordon Olivier. I'm the owner of Bookworm Books."

"And half the neighborhood," Adrian said, shaking the man's hand vigorously. "I look up to you, sir. In fact, I hope to *be* you someday." He kept pumping Gordon's hand. "I'm Adrian Stromquist."

Gordon looked over at me, his eyes twinkling. "I like this young man," he said. "He is your boyfriend?"

"No way," I said.

At the exact same time, Adrian answered, "Maybe."

"I understand perfectly," Gordon said with an eyebrow raise. "Do I smell coffee?"

"It's an old pot," Adrian said. "I've been awake for hours, working on some ideas. Come in, sit down, and I'll make you a fresh pot."

Gordon followed Adrian into the kitchen as though Adrian owned the place. Gordon placed his fedora on the stepstool-chair we kept off to the side, and took a seat at the table.

While Adrian made a fresh pot of coffee, Gordon started explaining his big plan to me.

Sales at the bookstore were steady but not great. He ran an analysis on the sales data and determined that eighty percent of our profits came from twenty percent of our stock.

"I could have told you that," I said. "It's the Pareto principle. It's true for almost every business. It's not exactly a sign we're doing anything wrong."

"So, you know the Pareto principle," Gordon said, smiling warmly.

Adrian called over his shoulder, "I know it, too. Eighty percent of your rewards come from twenty percent of your efforts."

"Then the genius of my idea should be immediately apparent to you," Gordon said. "We will be moving the bookstore to the vacant space next to Delilah's, and we will be turning the large, underutilized space into a specialty wine store."

I nodded, taking it all in. I'd heard variations on this idea before, so it wasn't exactly a head spinner.

Adrian brought Gordon a fresh mug of coffee and the fixings.

Gordon went on, detailing his plans. He'd already secured the proper licenses from the city. He'd even had a logo and branding designed for the wine store.

"But that space next to Delilah's is tiny," I said. "You haven't been able to get a tenant in there since the pop-up ice cream shop was there last summer." I remembered it well. That was the summer I'd switched from donuts to ice cream for a while. It was, not coincidentally, the same time my molar had started to bother me.

"I could have had a tenant if I'd wanted one," Gordon said lightly. "There are always dog groomers and consignment clothing shops." He wrinkled his nose. Gordon disliked those businesses because he felt they were the telltale sign of a building's value depreciating rapidly.

"Mr. Olivier, you'll have to suck it up and get one of those businesses in there," I said. "Bookworm Books won't fit. Customers would need a shoehorn to get themselves in the front door."

"We'll have to reduce inventory," Gordon said.

"If we reduce inventory, we reduce browsing time, which reduces sales. People come to a bookstore for something to do. They want to lose themselves. You can't get lost if you're wedged into a claustrophobic retail alley with no breathing room."

He replied calmly, as though he'd been expecting my argument, "The new space is small, but the ceiling is high. There is excellent airflow."

"We'd have to cut a third of our shelves."

Gordon gave me a steady look. He was seventy and had life experience I could only imagine.

"We'll need to cut forty percent," he said. "Fifty would be better."

"Impossible," I said, crossing my arms.

Adrian said, "It's the right move, Mr. Olivier. You need to maximize revenue for every square foot. Baker Street is a busy place, and it's only getting busier as the city grows. You'd probably be better off shuttering the bookstore permanently, but it's very generous of you to give it a chance to hang in there."

"Thank you," Gordon said.

I said nothing.

Gordon looked at me. "I'll hire someone to help you with the transition."

"Like a therapist?"

He smiled. "Perhaps. If you feel you need such a thing."

I gradually uncrossed my arms. It was hard to stay angry at Gordon Olivier. Between the French accent and his calm personality, there was so much to like about the older man.

"What you need is an operations manager," Adrian said. "Not just for moving the bookstore, but for setting up the wine shop. Do you have a layout for the interior?"

"Just the logo," Gordon said.

"Are you looking for someone for the job?"

Gordon smiled at Adrian. "I may have someone in mind. Are you available, Mr. Stromquist?"

"Actually, I am," Adrian said. "I've been going through some career transitions recently, but I'd love to take on something like this."

"Wait," I said, raising a hand. "If you hire Adrian as an operations manager, would that make him my boss?"

Gordon tilted his head back and forth in that noncommittal way of his.

Then the two of them began chatting about the timeline for the transition. Adrian gave Gordon two ideas that he loved instantly.

"You're hired," Gordon said.

And that was how Adrian Stromquist became my boss. Sort of.

Chapter 8

An Hour Later

Adrian and Gordon Olivier left my house together. They were chattering away happily, heading off to take some measurements and continue going over Mr. Olivier's plans for the bookstore move.

My hangover wasn't bad, thankfully.

I was concerned about my future but somewhat relieved the bookstore wasn't being shut down entirely. Losing half our shelves was going to suck, but I was already planning the inventory changes in my mind. Moving to a smaller location would be hard, but it would also shake things up. Shaking things up could be a good thing.

For example, our current space had a low ceiling, and it would be nice to be in a place with a high ceiling.

Nisha was always saying that the shape of a space affected your mood and thoughts. Being outdoors was the best for big, lofty thoughts, but having a higher ceiling over your head was also good. On the other hand, if you had to think about something tight and focused, it was good to be in a cozy space.

I was sitting at the table, daydreaming about paint colors, when Sunshine Banks emerged from Nisha's bedroom and padded her way into the kitchen, yawning sleepily. The tall, ringlet-haired young woman helped herself to the coffee without so much as a good morning.

I asked her, "How late were you guys at O'Flannigan's?"

"Too late," she said, stifling a yawn. "Brittany caught her second wind, and she made us do body shots. Tequila."

"Brittany is a wild girl," I said. "It sounds like I got out of there just in time."

She sat across the table from me and fixed me with her dark-brown eyes. "Did you sleep with Adrian?"

"He slept on the couch," I said lightly, though my skin prickled at the directness of her question.

"Are you sure about that?"

"Sunshine! You must have walked right past him when you guys got here."

"We did," she said. "He woke up and talked to us a bit. He seemed agitated."

"That's Adrian for you. Moody and broody."

Sunshine looked down at the table and twirled her tightly coiled hair around her finger. "Do you even care about Adrian?"

"Of course I do," I said. "He's a friend, like you and Brittany."

She looked up at me. "Not exactly like us, though."

"What are you driving at?"

She narrowed her dark eyes at me. "What happened between you two last night?"

"He walked me home from O'Flannigan's," I said. "We saw some raccoons and narrowly escaped with our lives. Then we got back here and made sausage rolls."

"Then what?"

"Then nothing," I said. It hadn't exactly been nothing, but that wasn't Sunshine's business. I would never tell her I'd put a sausage roll in my cleavage and taunted him with it. I would tell Nisha, for sure, but nobody else.

"Hmm." She frowned.

"If you must know, after we ate the sausage rolls, I went to the bathroom and threw up. By myself. I didn't see Adrian again last night. He told me through the bathroom door that he'd be on the couch."

"But if you hadn't gotten sick, you would have had sex with him." Her dark eyes were accusatory. "I saw how you were hanging off him last night when you left the pub."

I sighed. My hangover wasn't bad, but I did have one, and Sunshine's voice made my temples throb.

"You were all over him," she said. "Something could have happened last night."

"I don't know, Sunshine. Maybe he could have gotten some action if he'd played his cards right. What's your point? Is this because Brittany likes him?"

She frowned. "Who said anything about Brittany? Does she like him?"

"I don't know," I lied. I'd heard from Nisha that Brittany was interested, but that fact didn't seem like something Sunshine wanted to hear.

Was Sunshine also into Adrian? Wow. Talk about a mess. For Adrian. It was a good thing I wasn't interested in him. Not really. It often seemed like I was interested in him whenever we were in a kitchen together, but perhaps that was just a transference thing, where I transferred my love of flaky, pastry-type foods onto the guy. He did resemble a breadstick.

Sunshine sipped her coffee noisily and continued staring at me.

I asked, "Do you want some breakfast to go with the interrogation?"

"We're just talking," Sunshine said cattily.

"Right. Just talking," I repeated.

"Would you rather talk about your amazing new modeling career?"

I could sense a trap when I heard one. "No, thanks," I said.

"Good. Because some people don't appreciate having their noses rubbed in the fact they haven't done anything with their lives."

"Are you kidding, Sunshine? Honestly, are you kidding? Do you actually think I've been bragging to you guys about being the right kind of fat girl to sell overpriced underwear to other desperate girls like me?"

"Don't pretend you're not excited. You'd be out of here and living in LA or New York in a heartbeat if you got the chance." She sniffed. "You don't even care about us."

"Oh, please. You're just mad at me because things aren't working out in your life how you planned. I'm sorry you haven't been discovered yet, or whatever. Don't try to play it like I did something awful. I've done some terrible things, but I haven't done them to you, okay?"

She put her face in her hands and made a choking sound.

The noises got wetter sounding.

Oh, flaming bag of poo, she was crying, wasn't she?

I came around the table and patted her on the shoulder. "Sunshine, you're going to get your break."

She sobbed, "I'm a terrible, awful, selfish person."

I had a hard time arguing with that.

She sobbed, "You've always been so nice to me, Peaches. I want to be happy for you, but it's so hard.

You already have everything, and now you have Adrian, too?"

I kept patting her shoulder. "I'm definitely not into Adrian. He's too tall," I said. "He's just a crusty breadstick that looks good until you bite into it. Plus he has weirdly long legs, like a giraffe."

She stopped crying and looked over at me. Sunshine was one of those beautiful girls who looked even more stunning when she cried.

Sunshine sniffed and said, "He does have skinny legs."

"There are plenty of fish in the sea," I said. "Neither of us needs Stormy Weather Adrian. He can blow himself into some other girl's port."

Sunshine didn't seem so keen on my metaphor.

"Let's have pancakes," I said.

She nodded. "Okay."

There was a shuffling down the hall. Nisha wandered in like a zombie. A zombie who wore tie-dyed pajamas.

Nisha said, "Did someone say pancakes?"

Brittany bounced in right behind my roommate, looking as fresh as a daisy and kicking up one foot playfully. "I could eat some pancakes," Brittany said cheerfully. "Want me to make them?"

The three of us answered in chorus, "Yes!"

We had pancakes, plus more coffee. I told the girls about Mr. Gordon Olivier's surprise visit, the plan for the bookstore, and Adrian Stromquist's new position as operations manager.

Brittany said, "That's going to be so good for Adrian. He really needs something stable in his life right now."

"Sure," I said. "I'm glad it's so great for him."

"What Adrian needs is adventure," Sunshine said. "He burned out on real estate because he's too young to be all about work."

"Everything in balance," Brittany said in her usual chirpy way.

"All work and no fun isn't balanced," Sunshine said.

Nisha didn't say anything. I knew from the glazed-over expression on her face that she wasn't listening to the conversation at all. She was hungover and worried about her own future.

We had our pancakes, and they were amazing.

After the girls left, I checked that Nisha didn't need the bathroom right away, then I drew a bath.

I settled into the steaming tub.

Nisha came in, apologized, and went to use the toilet.

I said, "This is exactly why I asked you ten minutes ago if you needed to use the washroom."

"I didn't need to go ten minutes ago," she said.

I attempted to draw the shower curtain to give her some privacy, but the magnets were stuck firmly to the side of the tub and it seemed like too much effort.

Nisha said, "The hand towel is gone because Brittany used it to dry herself after her shower."

"Why would I care where the hand towel is?"

"Don't you think that's weird? She used one tiny hand towel on her whole body. I told her she could go ahead and use a bath sheet, but she said it would be wasteful." Nisha got up and flushed. "I don't think I could dry my chest with a hand towel, let alone my whole body."

"She's small," I said. "It was great when you guys were cheerleaders, and you tossed her in the air."

"It was." Nisha washed her hands then dried them on her jeans. She looked at me in the tub.

I said, "Take a picture. It will last longer."

She turned away and asked, "Do you ever wonder what it's like? To be like Brittany? To be what everyone wants in a girl? Small, white, and cheerful?"

"I'm two out of three," I said.

She snorted. "You're one out of three."

"Then we're even," I said. "You're also one out of three."

She paused by the door. "Does Sunshine like Adrian?"

"Yes. He's going to have to pick between her and Brittany, I guess."

"What about you?"

"I don't care who he picks. As long as they don't do it in my bed, that's their business."

Nisha turned to face me, narrowing her eyes at me. "Right," she said. "You don't care." She snorted. "Have a good bath."

She left me to my peaceful floating.

I soaked in the water and my own thoughts.

Had Brittany really dried her tiny body with a hand towel? What a show-off.

I looked down at my body in the tub. All my curves. Most of them were, as the saying goes, "in the right places," but I was far from perfect, and I knew it. I had always considered myself body neutral, with my positive feelings balancing out the negative ones. But I still had negative ones.

However, the longer I soaked in the tub that Sunday, the more at peace I felt with myself.

The thing about accepting your body, no matter where the curves are or aren't, is it's not a one-time thing. You don't pose for an advertising campaign and then magically become cured of any lingering negativity. There's no door you walk through one time and leave your worries behind.

You have to accept your body over and over again, every time some little thing happens to remind you that life isn't fair, and that other people don't walk around with the same jiggles and creases you have.

Some people can dry their tiny bodies off with a little hand towel. So what?

You smile at your face in the mirror and tell that girl you love her, big bath towel and all.

Chapter 9

It was official. The Quad Crew was back together.

The Quad Crew consisted of myself, Peaches Monroe, plus Nisha Patel, Brittany Brown, and Sunshine Banks.

Ever since our impromptu high school reunion, the four of us had been hanging out all the time.

When the weekend rolled around again, we met again to have drinks but no dinner at O'Flannigan's. That time, I paced myself better and stuck it out the whole evening.

The other girls crashed at our house again—this time Brittany bunked with me—and on Sunday morning, when we discovered that nobody had restocked the pancake mix since the previous weekend, we decided to go out for brunch, like civilized adults.

We went by Delilah's first. The line for brunch was way too long, and we weren't that patient.

We crossed Baker Street and went a few blocks farther to Pancake International. It was similar to the International House of Pancakes chain of restaurants, except all the furniture had been sourced from yard sales, none of the dishes matched, and they only had six laminated menus, so each table had to share one. Actually, they were nothing like IHOP, apart from serving pancakes.

I ordered the Elvis in Paris, which was crepes with peanut butter, bananas, and honey; bacon on the side. The other girls went even more over the top. What Pancake International lacked in menus and decoration, they made up for with their bubbling chocolate fountain.

We had finished ingesting one million calories when Sunshine pulled out her phone.

The other three of us squealed and yelled at her.

"Screw you guys," she said bitterly. "Screw you and your stupid rule."

"You're paying for the tip," Brittany said. "That's the rule. You touched your phone first."

Sunshine stuck out her tongue. "It wasn't even worth it," she said, pouting. "My last post didn't get any love." Sunshine was—surprise, surprise—obsessed with social media and her number of followers.

My phone started ringing.

It was the bookstore calling, plus Sunshine had already taken the hit and would be paying for the tip, so I answered.

Adrian said grumpily, "We're out of five-dollar bills. I need you to do a bank run."

"No way," I said. "You're the genius who wanted to open on Sunday so you could get a feel for the store, allegedly. You and I both knew you only did it to suck up to Gordon. Whatever's happening right now, it's all on you, so you can deal with the five-dollar-bill situation yourself. Byeeee!"

"Wait," he said. "I'd go to the bank myself, but people won't get out of the store. They all brought in takeout coffees and they're way too comfortable."

"That's Sunday afternoon for ya. In case you didn't pick it up from my tone, there's a big, fat told-ya-so in there, Mr. Stromquist."

At the mention of Adrian's name, I had the full attention of two other young women sitting at my table.

Adrian said in a hushed tone, "We need to get rid of the chairs. Browsing is fine, but this isn't a library."

"If you take away the chairs, they just sit on the floor. Trust me, chairs are better."

"I'm trapped," Adrian moaned. "Trapped here without any fives, which means I'll be out of everything else in just a couple of transactions."

"Think of the readers as allies, not adversaries. How many are in there right now?"

"Six."

"Six is good. Now pick the most trustworthy-looking one and tell them they're in charge for ten minutes."

Adrian snorted. "That's no way to run a business."

"I know that. But the definition of a business is an entity that makes profits. Bookworm Books is more like a cultural institution."

Sunshine, who was across the table from me, waved to get my attention. She asked, "Is that Adrian? Is he at the bookstore? We should go there."

Brittany said to me, "Tell him we're coming over. Hello, Adrian!"

Adrian heard the girls and asked, "Who's that? Is that Sunshine and Brittany?"

"Yes," I said. "Nisha's here, too."

"Tell them I said hi."

I did, and the two who were in love with him squealed and bounced.

I said into the phone, "Hey, I have a question for you. Back in high school, who were you more in love with? Brittany Brown or Sunshine Banks?"

Across the table from me, the girls looked horrified about my question, but also keenly interested in the answer. Both leaned in. Over the past week, they'd discovered that both of them were in love with Adrian. They were being surprisingly cool about it. By surprisingly cool, I mean they hadn't scratched each other's faces off... yet.

Adrian spoke warily. "Are they both there with you right now?"

"Yes."

"Then my answer is I think they're both amazing girls, but I have my eyes on someone else."

"But who did you like better in high school?"

"It's the same answer," he said. "You know who I'm talking about."

I felt heat rising in my skin. Adrian had been subtly flirting with me all week while we'd been working together on the plans for moving the store. The subtlety had recently been thrown out the window.

When I didn't answer, Adrian said, "If you girls come by, bring five-dollar bills."

"We're busy, Adrian. We've got shopping to do."

"I know you're at Pancake International. That's walking distance. Come by when you girls are done demolishing the chocolate fountain."

I glanced furtively around the small restaurant.

"How do you know where I am?" I whispered into the phone.

"Sunshine has been texting me," Adrian said. "And Brittany, too. I know all about your rule about no cell phones at breakfast. They've both been sneaking off to the bathroom to send me messages."

"You love this," I said.

"I don't hate it," he said. "But there's only one girl I want to see today. And it's the girl who's going to bring me a big stack of five-dollar bills."

"Fine, but you owe me."

"I'll pay you back in sausage rolls," he said. "This time, you can eat them out of *my* cleavage."

"What?" I got up from the table and ran for a private corner of the restaurant.

"Or you can nibble them from... my waistband."

I cupped my hand over the phone. "Need I remind you that you are technically my boss? This is highly inappropriate."

"If you hate it so much, hang up the phone."

I showed him. I did end the call. But only because my battery died.

The truth was, I had been flirting right back at Adrian all week, and I was loving every minute of it.

Chapter 10

Sunshine, Brittany, and Nisha went ahead to the bookstore while I stopped by the bank for the change Adrian wanted. We were lucky there was a nearby branch that was open limited hours on Sunday afternoons.

When I arrived back at the bookstore with plenty of small bills and rolls of coins, Adrian was entertaining the girls with a story about some idiot running through the forest in the dark.

He was saying, "And then Peaches tripped over a tree branch and wiped out on the path. She tried to blame poor, toothless Cujo for her clumsiness."

Apparently, the idiot being discussed was me. And Cujo was there, at the store, wagging his tail and getting fawned over by the girls.

"Excuse me," I said, pushing my way in the conversation. "I did not trip over a branch, Adrian. Your dog attacked me."

Adrian laughed and said, "Cujo can barely attack mushed-up dog food from a can."

"And he's such a cutie pie," Sunshine said in baby talk to the dog. "Cujo's a good boy."

Brittany rubbed the German shepherd's ears and also spoke baby talk at the dog. "Who's a big teddy bear? You are!"

Nisha wandered off and started picking up books, flipping to the last page, and reading the endings.

I plopped the money on the counter. "Here you go, Mr. Shopkeeper."

"Since you're here, can you help me with something on the computer?"

"It's my day off," I said grumpily.

"If you don't want to get put to work, you shouldn't come in," he said smugly. He turned to the girls, who were lavishing affection on Cujo—affection they would rather be lavishing on Adrian—and asked if they wouldn't mind giving the old German shepherd a walk. "He's got a small bladder," Adrian said.

The girls jumped at the opportunity. Nisha put her book-ruining rampage on hold and went with them.

I walked around behind the counter and showed Adrian what he had been doing wrong with the computer.

Adrian grinned and said, "Leave it to Peaches Monroe to always point out exactly what it is I'm doing wrong."

"If you hate it so much, you could try doing things the right way," I said. "There is a help screen on this software."

"I like it when you help me," he said, his voice thick and gruff. "Sharing a computer with you brings back memories."

He'd gotten close to me at the computer, and now he leaned his body around mine, spooning me.

I ducked under his arm and got away quickly, before I could melt into him. There were customers in the store. And I wasn't interested in Adrian. The flirting was fun, but it was just that. Fun. A distraction from the stress of the impending move.

I started to leave. "Behave yourself without me here," I said. "Have a good afternoon."

"You can't go yet. I have so many questions."

"Such as?"

"Half of the houseplants on top of the shelves are plastic, but all of them have been getting watered. Why?"

"We don't have any plastic plants," I said.

He gave me his trademark you're-an-idiot look. "Never mind. You just answered my question."

"I'm not a giant giraffe made out of breadsticks," I said. "I can't see into the tops of the plant pots like you can."

He gave me a hurt look. "I'm a giraffe? Made out of breadsticks?" He held one hand to his chest. "At least I don't put my half-sucked-on cough drops in the scissors drawer."

"Sometimes a whole cough drop is more than I need." I crossed my arms. "You didn't suck on them, did you?"

"Come here and smell my breath."

"No, thanks."

"When are we going to have our staff meeting?"

"News flash," I said. "We don't do staff meetings."

Adrian crossed his arms. His *muscular* arms. The guy really had filled out since high school. I was noticing it more than ever because he was wearing one of his old black T-shirts, for his favorite underrated band, Megasoystick. Back in the day, the black T-shirts had been loose on his scrawny frame. He filled them out now.

"Seven o'clock," he said.

"What?" He'd probably said a few things, but I'd missed most of it, because I'd been distracted by the shirt and his body.

"I'll swing home and grab my mom's car, then I'll come pick you up at your house," he said. "We'll go out somewhere."

"For a staff meeting?"

He glanced over the customers camped out near the magazines. "What else? We've got plenty to go over."

"Is Gordon Olivier coming?"

"Of course not. He hired me to take care of operations so he doesn't have to. Does seven work? Will you be done hanging out with the Quad Squad?"

"I think I can squeeze you in."

He waggled his fair, sun-bleached eyebrows. "You can squeeze me any way you want."

I had a déjà vu moment. Dalton Deangelo had said something very similar to me. Now I was thinking about Dalton. It was the third or fourth time I'd thought about the actor that day. Why couldn't I get him out of my head?

"Seven o'clock," Adrian said with authority, then he excused himself to go help a vertically challenged customer pull down a book from the top shelf. With his giraffe height, he could reach anything in the store without a stepladder.

I stood near the door for a moment, observing him as he chatted with the customer. He was new to bookselling, but he was already better than our typical new hire. He looked comfortable and seemed friendly with the customers.

He certainly was comfortable and friendly around me.

Maybe too comfortable and friendly.

I would have to wear extremely ugly underwear to the staff meeting that night, just to discourage any bad ideas that might pop into my head.

I left the store and located the girls in the dog park. Cujo had made friends with a pair of adorable Chihuahuas named Duke and Princess. Their owners told us a charming story about how they lived in a different part of town now, but they used to meet at the dog park, so they came back sometimes to revisit their memories. The guy looked like the crazy Russian who had run the pop-up ice cream shop on

Baker Street the summer before, but he was way more mellow and had only a mild accent.

The girls wanted to go shopping, but I bailed on them with the excuse that I had to do laundry.

I headed home on my own, dreading the task ahead of me. We didn't have a washer and dryer in the house, so laundry day meant lugging my stuff to the laundromat. I didn't have a car, so it was a huge undertaking involving a wheeled cart. Could I even get it done before putting on ugly underwear for my appointment with Adrian?

There was one other issue with my "staff meeting" at seven o'clock. I was supposed to be having dinner with my family right about that time.

When I got home, I called my mother and asked if I could reschedule.

She didn't like the sound of that. She said, "I was hoping to see you tonight, Peachy. I could use someone to talk to."

"Has Dad been using the bucket again?"

There was a pause. "It's not that. Are you busy this afternoon?"

"I should be doing laundry."

"I'll drive over and pick you up. You can do your laundry at the house."

"Are you sure? I can take it to the laundromat. It's a nice enough place. They have coffee."

She sighed on the other end of the line. "Peachy, do we have to go through this every time?"

"Yes," I said.

"Fine. I *insist* that you let your mother help you with your laundry," she said. "I'll be over in twenty minutes."

The truth was, in all the time I'd been living at the house with Nisha, I'd only hauled my stuff to the laundromat one time. The place was nice enough, and it did serve coffee, but it couldn't compete with the Monroe residence. My folks had top-of-the-line machines that handled oversized loads and didn't charge a penny, plus my mother loved folding.

Chapter 11

My mother helped me haul my laundry in through the back door, which was next to the laundry room.

I could hear at least two children running around inside the house.

My mother yelled out, "Elliot! The famous supermodel is here!"

Elliot Monroe had been told that his big sister was going to be doing some modeling soon, in her underwear. He'd taken it well. By which I mean he didn't care at all.

Elliot came charging through, chasing another little boy. The other boy held a big plastic shark high over his head.

The boys yelled excitedly, competing for my attention, then scampered off as quickly as they'd arrived.

My father appeared, said, "I'm getting too old for this," then disappeared after the boys.

Mom and I sorted my laundry. She admired all my fancy new underwear.

"I should have brought some back for you," I said. "Next time."

"This stuff is much too fancy for me," she said. Her eyes said otherwise.

Once we had a load going in the washing machine, we made a pot of tea and sat in the breakfast nook.

My mother hadn't brought up whatever it was that had been bothering her, so I asked.

She frowned into her teacup. "It's probably nothing. I get tired. Elliot's been such a handful lately."

I held up both hands. "No refunds. No take-backsies." That was our little joke whenever she complained about the kid.

She didn't even crack a smile. This was serious.

"Mom, do you want me to spend some more time with him and give you a break? He could come for an overnight at the house again. It's been a while since we had a sleepover. Nisha loves having him around, and he loves playing with all her crystals."

She didn't say anything.

I asked, "What's he doing, specifically?"

"Oh, just the usual kid stuff." She waved a hand. "Boys are not like girls. I've been comparing notes with Astrid, and it sounds like he's a lot like how Adrian was as a little boy." She looked up at me, her bright-blue eyes lined with red. She'd been crying, by the looks of it. "It's hard to be an only child," she said.

I held up both hands again. "No rain checks," I said, which was another one of our in-jokes. I made it whenever it sounded like my mother wanted another baby.

"Honestly, I wouldn't be able to handle another one." She straightened up. "No. I think we have it figured out. Elliot has some nice friends in the neighborhood, and we're going to invite them over more often for play dates, so that Elliot doesn't turn out like Adrian."

I was surprised to hear her saying something critical about Adrian. The way my parents talked about the guy, you'd think the sun rose and set on Adrian Stromquist.

"What do you mean?" I asked. "What's wrong with Adrian?" I added, "Besides the obvious, that he's a smug know-it-all."

"You know how he can be," she said, nodding her head to the side. "Adrian had a hard time growing up. It's tough to have a cop for a father. According to Astrid, he didn't make friends easily, and he was alone a lot. Then he went off on that ambitious career journey of his, and he burned out because he didn't have any support. A person needs support in their life."

"You and Astrid have been talking a lot."

"She needs a friend," my mother said. "She's not very happy about having Adrian back home. She's worried about his self-destructive nature."

"His *what*? Astrid needs to get out more and talk to actual twenty-somethings. Adrian is not exactly imploding. Do you know what he drinks at O'Flannigan's when he goes there with his laptop to work on his screenplay? Non-alcoholic beer. Does that sound self-destructive to you?"

"People self-destruct in different ways." She got up. "We need cookies. What was I thinking? You can't serve tea without cookies."

She returned with a selection of homemade cookies.

I asked, "Is this what you wanted to talk to me about? You and Astrid are worried about Elliot turning out like Adrian? A weirdo loner who drinks nonalcoholic beer in a pub with his laptop? A person could do worse."

She bit into a cookie. "When you say it like that, it sounds ridiculous. They have their similarities, but Elliot is already much more social than Adrian was at that age."

"He's not a clone, Mom. He's his own person."

"I know."

"Plus you and Dad are doing an amazing job. He's going to turn out great."

My mother visibly relaxed. "Thanks. It helps to hear someone say that." She fussed around with some crumbs on her plate. "What do you think of those face treatments women get? The fillers, and the Botox?"

I leaned back in my chair. "What did Dad do now?"

"It's not your father." She looked away and squeezed her eyes closed as she spat out, "A woman at the summer camp meeting thought I was Elliot's *grandmother*."

I could have said that—technically—it was true. I bit my tongue.

Instead of stating the obvious, I said, "Tell me who it was, and I'll punch her some new freckles."

"I don't even know her name. She's one of those perfect, stylish types. She's all over social media, and all the other moms follow her."

"I hate her already," I said. "Does she drive a ridiculously large vehicle and wear ridiculously tiny jeans?"

My mother grinned. "Not jeans. Yoga pants. The designer kind, though."

"Yoga pants. Uh-huh. With perfect hair and full makeup? Even in the morning?"

"Plus diamond earrings."

I shook my head. "Don't you worry about her. Those ladies have it the worst. I see them at the bookstore all the time. They're always buying diet and self-help books about being happy. They put on a good show, but they're very hard on themselves. Us regular ladies have to be kind to them, because those strung-out super-achievers need compassion more than anyone." I picked at the cookie crumbs. "Wow. That meditation must be kicking in. I sounded like Nisha for a minute."

My mother sighed. "It was just the way she looked at me, you know?"

"It's perfectly understandable that you'd be feeling rattled by something like that." I ate a cookie and looked at my mother. "You don't need to do anything to your face. I showed Mitchell some pictures of you, and he wants you to come in and shoot with me next year for a Mother's Day campaign."

My mother laughed off the suggestion. "I can't model underwear. I've got my hands full. I can't even get my son to flush the toilet after he uses it."

The two boys entered the kitchen, dressed in superhero pajamas. Their little nostrils flared.

"Cookies," Elliot said, pointing an accusatory finger.

His friend held back, digging in his nose with absolutely no shame. Ah, to be seven again.

My mother and I slid over and invited the boys to join us for one cookie.

"We only eat one," my mother said, picking up what I knew very well was her third cookie.

I wiped the crumbs off my plate discreetly and picked up another one, too. "I'm going to have my *one* cookie now," I said to the boys.

Elliot gave me one of Adrian's smug, know-it-all grins. "Liar," he said. "I can smell cookies on your breath, Pee-Pee."

My mother and I exchanged a look. What were you supposed to do when your kid caught you lying?

I handed him a cookie and changed the subject. "What superhero are you?"

He answered with the creativity typical of a seven-year-old, and then his friend did the same.

The four of us had an excellent conversation about superpowers. My mother worked in the fact that superheroes always flushed the toilet after they were done using it.

I put my arm around the kid and hugged him to my side.

I had no idea if I would have felt differently toward Elliot if he'd been my little brother, and not the child I'd given birth to. I'd never had a brother, so how would I know to compare? I did love the little guy. I loved every hair on his head. He was a sweetheart. Who wouldn't?

He'd never nursed from me. Despite understanding the health benefits, I hadn't been emotionally able to do it. My parents had assured me it was okay, and we all believed it might have made it easier for my parents to bond with him as their own.

Still, there were times, such as when I was with him and another boy his age, that I would compare.

Was the other boy taller or stronger? Did Elliot's friend seem smarter, having benefited from prenatal care? Comparison was the thief of joy, but we all did it. With our children, our appearances, and even with our lives. We were always comparing our insides to other people's outsides.

Elliot's friend finished his cookie and resumed digging in his nose without any self-awareness.

Elliot gave his friend a dirty look. "Gross," he said.

I was so relieved. Clearly Elliot was the champion kid so far.

The boys grew bored of the interaction and ran off to continue their adventures.

My mother began to cry, smiling through the tears. "I'm so blessed," she said. "So what if I have some wrinkles? I have two beautiful children who make me happy."

"And one of us knows how to flush a toilet."

She wiped her eyes. "Now that I'm done feeling sorry for myself, what's going on with you? What do you and Nisha have planned for tonight?"

"I've actually got a date," I said.

Breathlessly, she said, "He's back. Dalton's back. I knew it."

"Don't get too excited," I said. "It's not Dalton, and it's not an actual date. I misspoke. I have a staff meeting."

She frowned. "On a Sunday night?"

"There's a lot to go over, with the store move and everything."

"But that doesn't sound like a very fun way to spend your evening. I hope Mr. Olivier is paying you for your time."

"He won't be there. It's a staff meeting with me and our operations manager, Adrian."

"Oh." She pulled her head back. "Don't tell him anything about what I said about him. I wouldn't want to hurt his feelings."

"It's pretty hard to hurt Adrian's feelings," I said. "He may have been a loner with no friends, but he's weirdly confident in himself."

"He does have a near-genius IQ."

I rolled my eyes. "According to his mother, right?"

"He really does," she said earnestly. "They had him tested and everything."

"Does Adrian know about this supposedly high IQ?"

"Of course. He could have had much better marks in school if he hadn't been so committed to feeling sorry for himself and listening to that band. What was it called? Drumstick Bones?"

"Megasoystick," I said.

"Right."

"He's got a high IQ and knows it, huh? That actually explains a lot about Adrian." I rubbed my chin. "Very interesting."

"Elliot is also very smart," she said.

"Except when it comes to flushing the toilet."

She smiled knowingly and leaned back. My mother had a bit of a smug, know-it-all look herself sometimes. "Yes, well, we all have our blind spots, Peachy."

Chapter 12

My mother dropped me and my clean laundry off at the house.

I did not put on ugly underwear for the staff meeting with Adrian Stromquist. I couldn't. I'd thrown out every last piece to make room in my drawers for the bounty of new lacy, silky things I'd gotten from my modeling gig.

Since my underwear was so fancy, I pulled on an orange-colored wrap dress I'd picked up in LA.

I'd only wanted to see how the dress looked. I hadn't been planning to wear it for my staff meeting. The tight-fitting garment hugged every curve and left little to the imagination. Wearing a dress like that to a business meeting with my boss would have been highly inappropriate.

However, I happened to still be wearing the dress when Adrian arrived at seven o'clock, and I didn't want to keep him waiting, so I pulled on some sandals and took one last look in the mirror.

I thought of a Coco Chanel tip that Mitchell had drummed into my head in LA. *Before you leave the house, look in the mirror and remove one accessory.*

I heard Mitchell's voice in my head. "Honey, you don't need earrings *and* a necklace, do you?"

No, Mitchell, I did not. I took off the necklace.

Adrian knocked on the door again.

I yelled for him to hold his horses, then ran out and opened the door.

Adrian stood on the porch looking at the street, his back to me. He looked even taller from behind. He was wearing his usual jeans and black T-shirt. If there'd been a businesswear version of Adrian back in his real estate days, he'd left all his suits behind.

A summer breeze blew a vaguely citrus scent from his body to my nose. I liked it.

"Yo, Adrian," I said, using the voice from the Rocky movies that Adrian had always hated.

He turned around, saw me, and his icy blue eyes opened wide. "You look like a girl," he said.

"I am a girl."

"So people keep telling me."

"What people?"

"My mother, for one."

"How is your mother? She hasn't been spreading rumors about us again, has she?"

Adrian lost control over his eyes. They dropped and locked onto my chest.

I waved my hand in front of my chest. "Are you looking for sausage rolls, or are you eye-groping my sweater puppies?"

"Busted," he said, forcing his chin up and giving me a guilty look. "I'm always on the hunt for sausage rolls."

I pulled the top of my dress out and peered down. "None have shown up here yet, but you never know."

"We can check later." He glanced behind me. "They're not here, are they?"

"Your groupies? No. They've gone back to their respective homes. I didn't tell them you were coming by, or they'd be here now, offering to get your mom's car detailed for you. When are you going to put them out of their misery and pick one?"

His fair eyes twinkled as he rubbed one hand over his mouth and down his long, angular features. "Why would I have to pick just one?"

"It's only fair," I said.

"Which one would you pick?"

"That's a tough one. Sunshine's the right height for you, and she's a sarcastic know-it-all, like you, which nobody likes. Brittany's way more agreeable, but she's a cheap drunk, and she does kick her foot up like this when she gets excited." I kicked up my foot behind me.

"It's cute when you do it," he said.

"So pick Brittany."

"We'll see," he said. "It's only June. Cuffing season doesn't start until October. By then, I'll have a better idea about what I need to keep me warm through the chilly winter months."

I rolled my eyes. "Ugh. Cuffing season. I hate that term."

"Maybe you won't hate it this year."

I put my hands on my hips. "Are we going somewhere for this staff meeting, or what?"

"Right this way," he said, gesturing for me to follow him.

He had driven his mom's car over, as he'd promised. Cujo was in the back seat, wagging his tail happily when I got in the front.

As we drove away, I didn't want to compare my date with Adrian to my dates with Dalton, but I did. Adrian came with his mother's old car and a toothless German shepherd. Dalton came with a fancy vehicle and a butler driver. The guys couldn't be more different.

But driving away from my house with either one of them made my heart flutter the same amount.

Chapter 13

Adrian drove us to the Pier, a popular tourist destination with a boardwalk on the waterfront. The place was packed all summer long, and that Sunday was no exception.

We walked along with Cujo loping alongside us, attracting a lot of attention from young women.

"This dog is a lady killer," I said to Adrian.

"He takes after me," Adrian said, pretending to buff his nails on his shoulder.

We had our choice of dinner places. We opted for takeout fish and chips that we took outside to the picnic tables, where we could sit with Cujo and eat our food while seagulls watched us sulkily. There were multiple signs all over the place begging people not to feed the seagulls, but the seagulls couldn't read.

"This is so good," Adrian said over his mouthful of battered and deep-fried cod. "It's even better than I remember. I don't even know the name of this place, but I used to come here all the time. I'm so glad it didn't change while I was away."

"Your whole summer is one big high-school reunion, isn't it?"

He nodded. "I've been revisiting a lot of old favorites."

"You sure have," I said.

He gave me a sexy look.

I cleared my throat. "We can start our staff meeting anytime."

He set down his cod and held up both hands. "So, here's what I want to do," he said. Then he outlined a pretty good plan in which we would have both locations open at the same time, while running a citywide literary scavenger hunt to get traffic in the old store and the new store, as well as free publicity. "Plus some paid publicity through the radio station," he added at the end. His blue eyes glinted with a ferocity I'd never seen before.

"You sound excited."

"I am," he said. "I know it's just a bookstore, but the principles of hype and sales are the same in any business."

"You love this stuff."

He smiled and looked away. "Whenever we were launching a new development project, I used to get so keyed up. I couldn't sleep. It was like a drug. The bigger the risk, the more excited I got. I was a degenerate addict, except the socially acceptable kind."

"That does check out with what I know of the business world." I had finished my fish and moved on to the fries.

Adrian wolfed down his fish in a few bites. "What about you? You were the smartest girl in school."

"What about you? My mom told me that her mom told her that you have a near-genius IQ. They had you tested and everything."

Adrian wrinkled his nose. "You can't trust those tests. They're biased toward a certain kind of intelligence."

"The kind you have," I said. "You were probably the smartest kid in school, not me."

He gave me a smug, know-it-all look. "That's why I specified that you were the smartest *girl*."

"I see."

"You were," he said. "And you would have been an excellent valedictorian, if that sly redhead hadn't stolen it from you."

"Ugh. We hate her. By we, I mean me and Nisha."

"Her speech was... interesting," Adrian said.

"It was awful," I said. "She started off by quoting lyrics from a Jade song. I think she meant to be ironic, but it was just embarrassing for everyone who had to sit through it."

Adrian leaned back, grinning like the cat who'd eaten the canary. "You don't know, do you?"

"Know what?"

"Her family bought her the valedictorian honor. Her dad paid off some people with a generous donation to the school's expansion fund."

I smacked my fist on the picnic table. "Shut up!"

Adrian smacked his own fist on the table, mimicking me. "Anywhere there's power and money, there's corruption."

"How do you know this?"

"I have no hard evidence, but I had my suspicions, so I ran my own polls. Most of the students actually voted for you."

"Are you sure? I didn't think people liked me that much."

"People liked you a lot more than you thought. More importantly, they knew you were the smartest girl in the class."

"I'm reeling, Adrian. I'm literally reeling from this information. I should have been the valedictorian. *Me*." I patted my cheeks with both hands. "Just think. My whole life could have been different."

"The redhead may have done you a favor. She went off to New York with all those class valedictorian expectations hanging over her. I bet every time she stumbled, she got that Impostor Syndrome thing. That's where you feel like a fraud, and that they're going to catch on to you." Adrian looked down at his empty takeout basket. His face took on the brooding look I knew so well.

"Adrian, did you have that Impostor Syndrome?"

He jerked his head up and grinned. "Nope. I guess that makes me a monster. I always felt I deserved every bit of success."

"Of course you did. Was there a girlfriend? You told me you had a big house with a pool, but you were lonely."

He stared into my eyes. "I didn't have time for a girlfriend. I was too busy obsessing over making a name for myself. I lost track of what mattered."

His gaze was too intense. I looked down and pointed to his rock band T-shirt. "Why Megasoystick? Why them?"

"Honestly, I liked the same music as everyone else. I wore these shirts because nobody else did, and I thought it made me seem interesting. That and the lip ring. A kid's gotta do something to distance himself from his dad, the cop. It's hard being a cop's kid."

"I never thought of you as a cop's kid. You were just Adrian. With your spider legs and your floppy hair, always looking for a rain cloud to sit underneath. You didn't have a lot of guy friends, did you? You were always alone."

"Ouch. It hurts because it's true."

"Being alone is okay sometimes."

"The upside to being a loner is you don't get much peer pressure. I never even smoked a cigarette, let alone anything more interesting. A lot of cop's kids are way more rebellious."

"Do you think people left you out because they thought you'd snitch to your dad?"

"The irony is that, thanks to my dad, I knew who all the dealers were, and where the bootleggers operated. I had all that info but didn't know what to do with it."

"You could have been the most popular guy in school."

He nodded, his expression wistful. "And you could have been valedictorian, except for a certain redhead and her father's bribe money."

A quiet moment passed. The seagulls, sensing our lapsed attention, drew closer.

Cujo jumped up and chased off the birds, slobbering and barking. Mostly slobbering.

Adrian watched the dog and flicked at his lower lip with his tongue. He had no piercing anymore, but the flicking gesture took me back in time. I used to watch him flick that piercing and wonder what it would be like to kiss him. Until I did. The piercing had been interesting, but not as fascinating as the rest of him.

I asked, "When did you take the lip ring out?"

"The day I left this city. On my way out, I saw a bunch of skinny kids with piercings hanging around outside the bus station. When I walked by, they nodded at me like I was one of them."

"Street kids?"

"Yes. But I wasn't one of them. I had an internship and an apartment lined up. I slipped the lip ring out about two blocks later."

"Did the hole in your lip completely close up?"

He batted his eyelashes at me. "Wanna find out for yourself?"

"Pass."

He got up from his seat. "Good staff meeting. Let's go do something fun."

I finished my last french fry and got up. "Like what?"

"I'm going to take you somewhere we should have gone years ago."

I gave him a wary look. "To the drugstore to purchase birth control?"

"Somewhere else we should have gone." He gave me a teasing grin. "You don't know?"

"I have no idea. You want to listen to music? Get ice cream? Go dancing?"

"Funny you should say that. I know a place where we can do all three of those things."

"I have no idea what you're talking about."

He raised his eyebrows and waited.

The answer came to me in waves. There was one particular date activity Adrian had insisted on putting in the script we'd written in high school. It was a sport for the main characters to participate in. Adrian believed it was the ultimate tentpole scene. It would look dynamic in the movie trailer, plus almost anything could happen. The location supported action, movement, drama, fancy lighting, and the best songs on the soundtrack.

I looked into his eager eyes and said, "Roller skating."

He grinned. "Roller skating," he said.

Chapter 14

It turned out that rollerskating was fun, but not quite as fun as Adrian and I had hyped it up in our high school screenplay.

We turned in our skates after only forty minutes, even though we'd paid for two hours.

The sun was setting and the sky was purple when we walked out of the roller rink and back to Adrian's mother's car, where Cujo was waiting with all the windows rolled down.

Adrian said to me, "Roller skating is way harder than it looks in the movies. My legs are shaking right now."

"You must be weak," I teased. "My legs aren't shaking at all."

"That's because you spent most of our skate session on your butt, trying to drag me down with you."

"You're the one who wanted to do that thing where you pulled me through your legs. Once I got down there, it was hard to get back up again."

"You're not supposed to sit down during that move," he said. "You do a deep squat, resting on your heels, like this." He demonstrated, then groaned as he got back up again.

"See? It's hard to come up from that. You know, we would have discovered the truth about roller skating if we'd done our research back in the day."

We reached the car, and he opened the passenger side door for me.

"We did the important research," he said. He leaned in toward me. I sensed an incoming kiss, so I quickly slid into the seat.

I received slobbery kisses from Cujo, who must have thought we'd abandoned him forever, having been gone over forty-five minutes.

The kisses weren't enough for Cujo, who climbed over the armrest and got in my lap. Have I mentioned Cujo was a German shepherd? Not exactly a lap dog.

"He likes to ride up front lately," Adrian said, laughing. "You're in his seat."

I opened the door, extracted myself from underneath the dog, and climbed into the back.

"Much better," I said from the back seat. "Take me home, Bernard."

Adrian glanced back at me. "Bernard? What kind of a name is that for a chauffeur? Isn't it supposed to be James?"

"Sure," I said. "Take me home, James."

Adrian stared at me, his eyes narrowing. "Bernard is the name of that guy who drove *him* around, isn't it? Nisha said he was a butler or something. She couldn't place his accent, but she said it was legit. I have a good memory for names, and I know she said it was Bernard."

"You are too smart for your own good," I said. "You got me. Bernard was the butler."

Adrian kept staring. "You're not thinking about *him* when you're with me, are you?"

"I'm not *with* you, Adrian. We're friends and coworkers. You're currently my boss."

"You and I both know I'm not your boss. Peaches Monroe answers to nobody. She has no boss."

He had me there.

He turned around and started driving.

When we got to my house, he jumped out and opened my door for me, chauffeur style. "Ma'am," he said.

"Thank you, driver."

We stood on the sidewalk facing each other. Well, I was facing his Adam's apple. Adrian Stromquist wasn't a giant giraffe made out of breadsticks, but he was tall.

He looked down at me. "Thanks for being so supportive of my ideas for the big relaunch with the bookstore."

"Who said I was supportive?"

"You didn't argue with me at all when I told you the plan. Maybe you've changed in the last five years, but that used to be a good sign you believed in my ideas."

"It's a good plan," I said.

The sky was purple over our heads. The weather was warm. We'd just had a very enjoyable time together. I wasn't sure about inviting Adrian inside, but I didn't want things to end just yet. The mood was very romantic.

He grinned down at me. "I've got a lot of good plans. Should I come inside and tell you about the other ones?"

I chewed my lip. "Do your plans involve you seeing the fancy underwear I'm wearing underneath this dress?"

He was about to answer when someone else said, "Oh, dear."

We both turned to find Mr. Galloway, my seventy-something neighbor, standing five feet away and looking scandalized. He must have overheard us.

"Hi, Mr. Galloway," I said. "This is my friend, Adrian Stromquist. He's been working for Mr. Olivier at the bookstore."

The older man's eyebrows went up. "Is that so?"

"And I've got good news for you," I said. "Baker Street is getting that specialty wine shop after all. It's happening this summer, if everything goes as planned by our incredible operations manager, who happens to be this tall drink of water right here."

Adrian repeated his name and shook Mr. Galloway's hand.

My neighbor continued to stand there, wringing his hands.

So much for the romantic mood. I loved my chatty neighbors, but they could be chatty at the wrong times.

"You're outside late," I said to the older man. "Is something going on with your roses?"

"It's the rat," Mr. Galloway said. "Oh, it's just... I can't even say it." He glanced over at his front door and shuddered visibly.

I looked over at Adrian, who appeared to be as concerned as I felt.

Adrian asked, "What's happening?"

Mr. Galloway shook his head, nodded his head forward, and held up one hand.

I took him by the elbow. "Mr. Galloway, would you like to come inside my place for a minute? You look like you could use a cup of tea or something."

He raised his head with effort and pushed his glasses up his long, thin nose. "If you don't mind," he said weakly. "I am feeling a bit rattled."

We went inside the house. Nisha wasn't home, so I ran around flicking on lights.

I desperately needed to freshen up, so I excused myself for a moment.

When I got back out to the kitchen, Adrian had taken control of the situation and was extracting the story from my neighbor.

In short, Mr. Galloway's battle with the rat who'd been terrorizing him in his house had reached its climax. The final skirmish was at hand, no thanks to his cat, who'd made friends with the rat.

But victory was not to come easy. The rat was not yet deceased. It had been injured by the trap, and was making horrible noises, still alive and trapped under Mr. Galloway's refrigerator. The cat was upset about what was to happen to its friend, so the cat was standing guard in the kitchen.

My neighbor, a gentle man who wouldn't hurt a fly, was beside himself. Tears ran down his cheeks.

"I'm not a killer," he said.

Adrian got up from his chair, looking almost as pale as my elderly neighbor.

"I'll take care of it," he said grimly. "That's the house on this side?" He pointed in the correct direction.

We both nodded silently.

Adrian left.

Mr. Galloway and I sat in silence, waiting. The sun was finishing for the day. The room was bathed in a golden-orange light that seemed too cheerful for the occasion.

I found myself listening for any signs of screaming or banging from next door.

After eleven minutes and twenty seconds, Adrian returned, his expression solemn.

"Everything's been taken care of," he said with no emotion.

I helped Mr. Galloway to his feet. I walked him back over to his house while Adrian stayed behind.

Mr. Galloway patted my arm when we reached his front door. "You're a true friend," he said.

His tears were gone, but his discomfort remained. Mr. Galloway wasn't from a generation that condoned grown men crying—not that things were wildly different today.

"I'm sure we'll laugh about this someday," I said. "But if you'd prefer, I will never, ever mention it."

He looked down at his feet. "Thank your friend for me," he said. "He's a good man."

"He is," I agreed.

Mr. Galloway quietly slipped inside his house and closed the door.

Adrian met me on my porch, looking anxious. "I should get going," he said, rubbing his bare forearms.

I wanted to say something to make everything fun and romantic again, but the evening had taken a turn. There was no salvaging it. You can't do a U-turn from extermination back to kissing.

"It is late," I said. "Plus I have to work in the morning, and it will take me hours to sort out everything you probably messed up today."

He blinked at me. "You may have to restock your supply of half-sucked-on cough drops."

"Like I said, it'll be a busy morning for me."

"See you around," he said, and then he went to his mother's car.

When Adrian opened the driver's side door, Cujo must have felt it was time for a walk. He threw himself out of the car like a puppy. Then the elderly dog refused to get back in the car. He had a lot of things to smell and tinkle on.

Adrian stood by, waiting patiently. He and I made increasingly awkward conversation about half-sucked-on cough drops, then he left.

Chapter 15

Monday, June 20th

Rhonda steamed the milk for my mocha while she complained about the customers at the bookstore. Rhonda had filled in for me at Bookworm Books during my week away in Los Angeles. I'd been back for over a week, but I'd been keeping away from deep-fried pastries. Posing in one's underwear for a week straight can temporarily dampen one's enthusiasm for starches. I hadn't been in to properly catch up with the woman until that Monday morning.

"Nothing's ever simple with those book customers of yours," Rhonda said in the gravelly voice that made her seem a lot older than she was. "Don't get me wrong. It was a nice change of pace for me, but I'll stick to donuts and coffee."

I pulled up a stool to the counter. "Were they really that hard on you?"

"I'm sure they didn't mean to be," she said. "It's just not something I'm used to. The people who come into Donut Joe's know exactly what they're going to get, and they're fine with that. They don't look to me for guidance. They don't ask me what they should pick, like I'm supposed to be their fairy godmother of literature." She poured the steamed milk into my cup. "Do I look like a woman who has all the answers to the mysteries of life?"

"Kind of," I said. "You do have a certain wisdom about you."

"It's the voice," she said. "And before you say anything, you should know it was like this long before I ever smoked. I had this voice when I was five. It was awful. Whenever we got a substitute teacher, they thought I was playing a prank and sent me to the principal's office." Rhonda grinned. "Actually, I liked that part. It's fun to get in trouble when you haven't done anything wrong, because then everyone has to apologize to you."

"I wouldn't know what that's like," I said. "When I get in trouble, it's usually my own fault."

She handed me my mocha. "Speaking of trouble, what's happening with you and the actor? Is it true you split up?"

"We're not together," I said.

She leaned forward and looked over the counter at me, from head to toe. "If you're not with the actor, then who is this for?"

I was wearing another one of the form-fitting dresses I'd picked up in LA. "Can't a girl dress up for work?"

Rhonda gave me a knowing look. It wasn't just her voice that made her seem wise. Rhonda also had the facial expressions of a woman who'd seen it all.

"There might be someone," I said. "He's helping out at the bookstore. Gordon Olivier has big plans. It's not official yet, but we're moving the bookstore to the spot next to Delilah's. The overhead is lower, so it will help us weather any financial ups and downs. These days, you never know when the next calamity is about to hit."

"As long Mr. Olivier doesn't raise the rent too much on this place," Rhonda said. "Wait. When you say someone's working with you on the move, do you mean the tall blond guy who looks like this?" She sucked in her cheeks and made a bored face.

"I see you've met Adrian Stromquist," I said.

She raised her eyebrows. "Not bad, Peaches. Not bad at all."

"He took me roller skating last night."

"Romantic."

"Not how I do it."

"Did you hook up?"

"No. It was feeling like we might become more than friends, except he had to kill a rat for my neighbor. It ruined the mood. It's hard to make a smooth transition from murder to romance."

"It sure is," she said, a little too knowingly.

"Maybe it was for the best that nothing happened last night," I said. "We have to work together. We should keep things professional."

"Plus your actor guy is back in town," she said.

He was? My ears pricked up.

Rhonda said, "Maybe you two can patch things up. I watched some of his supernatural TV show last night. I got curious after he was in here during the day. The show's not the best, but I believe I understand the man's appeal much better now."

"Dalton was here? Yesterday?"

"He was. He had green tea and a donut."

"Oh. You must be mistaken. Dalton Deangelo would never eat a donut."

"He *ordered* a donut. He only ate half."

"You're sure it was him?"

"Dark hair, thick eyelashes, and green eyes like emeralds? It was him. Some of my regulars who come in on Sunday afternoons—Gloria and Skyler—got their pictures taken with him." Rhonda fixed the tie on her apron and stared off dreamily. "He's very warm with his fans. What a guy."

"What a guy," I said coolly. "He flashes that sexy smile and gets anything he wants."

I paid for the mocha and left to open the bookstore.

As I walked next door, I expected to find a TV vampire lurking in the doorway waiting for me.

Nobody was there.

I can't say I wasn't a little disappointed.

Chapter 16

For the rest of that Monday morning, my mind was on Dalton Deangelo.

I barely had the mental energy to get annoyed at all the things Adrian had messed up or moved around the day before.

About two hours into my shift, though, I was cursing Adrian's name. Not only had my new operations manager thrown away my half-sucked-on cough drops, but he'd messed up the special filing system I'd been using for invoices. What once had been an impressive tower of paper with everything how I liked it was now a smug little filing cabinet—yes, filing cabinets could be smug—with color-coded file folders. Adrian had even left passive-aggressive notes about how to file things. According to him, I was some sort of monster who had to be told that alphabetical meant *by the alphabet*.

I might have called Adrian and chewed him out properly, but a man with dark hair walked by the front windows, and my mind zipped back to a certain sexy actor. It wasn't Dalton, but now my focus was back on him.

Had the actor who played the smoldering Sir Drake Cheshire really been at Donut Joe's the day before, risking his personal trainer's wrath by eating half a donut?

I checked online and confirmed—as best I could, considering it was the internet—that Dalton Deangelo was, indeed, back in the city. The movie production team had picked up shooting on *Waterfall*, with rumors of massive script changes.

"Good," I said to my phone screen. "Better yet, burn it."

A white-haired woman who'd been standing nearby jumped.

"Sorry," I said to her. "You're so quiet. I thought I was alone in here."

She leaned over, looked behind the counter, then gave me a disappointed look. "He's not here," she said, more to herself than to me.

"Are you looking for the blond guy who was working here yesterday? Tell me what he did wrong and I'll write him a note," I said.

"Not him," she said. "The dog. I was hoping to see Cujo. I brought him a treat." She pulled a dog biscuit from her purse. "It's from a local bakery. It's a soft one, so..." She trailed off, looking embarrassed.

"That's sweet of you," I said. "You got a soft one because Cujo doesn't have any teeth." I accepted the dog biscuit. "I'll pass this on, along with your regards." I recognized the woman but didn't know her name. I offered my hand. "I'm Peaches," I said.

"Carla," the woman said. "I'm not crazy."

I replied, "Neither am I."

"Cujo reminds me of my dog, Max. It's been a couple of years since he went over the rainbow bridge, but I still miss him. German shepherds are the most wonderful animals."

"I'm sure they are," I said. "Cujo and I had a strange first encounter. He tackled me in the woods because he thought I was a perp. But the furry guy has grown on me." I looked down at the biscuit. "That looks tasty," I said. "Peanut butter?"

She gently took the dog biscuit back from me. "If you don't mind, I'll come back another time, when Cujo's here."

"Carla, do I look like the kind of woman who eats dog biscuits?"

"Of course not," she said, horrified. She tried to hand it back to me again. I laughed about it—she seemed like a sweet lady who meant well—and insisted she hang onto the special biscuit for her next visit. "Then Cujo can drool on you directly instead of through me," I said.

Carla thanked me and left the bookstore.

I still had my phone handy, so I sent Adrian a quick text message to let him know that not only did he have groupies, but Cujo did, too.

He received the message but didn't reply.

Lunch time came and went.

Customers popped in, browsed, chatted about books, bought a few, and left.

My father came by to check that I didn't have the air conditioner set too high.

As he was fiddling with the settings, he said, "I got a copy of that contract of yours by email."

"Finally," I said. "And? How bad is it? Did I sign away my soul? My firstborn? Too late for that one."

"You *did* sign your soul away," he said matter-of-factly.

"Don't joke around. When you get serious like this, I get worried."

"Then you should have read it before you signed it," he said. "You basically agreed to do anything and everything the actor's people deem necessary to mitigate any potential damage to Mr. Deangelo's reputation."

"Such as?"

"I don't know. It wasn't specified. It could mean anything. That's the whole point of a blanket promise to do 'anything and everything.' It's not something I would ever put in a warranty agreement for my products. That's a hole big enough to drive an M1 Abrams through." He added, "That's a tank."

"I figured it out from the context," I said.

"Let's hope these people don't want an M1 Abrams from you."

"Let's hope," I agreed. I couldn't imagine what a tank-sized favor would be. I'd already posed nearly nude for those people. How much more could they possibly want?

My father said, "At least the contract specifies that you will be fairly compensated."

"Oh, phew," I said. "So I'll get paid if I have to, say, make an appearance somewhere. That's not so bad. I can live with that. It's not like I have to, you know, marry the guy for the sake of the photo ops."

My father headed toward the door and paused to point a finger my way. "Don't sign anything else."

"Only autographs," I promised.

After my dad left, I looked around for something to take my mind off Dalton and the NDA contract.

It didn't take me long to think of a compelling activity to keep my hands busy and my mind occupied.

I located the collection of sparkly stickers I'd had stashed away for a rainy day, fired up the color printer, and got to work on a series of small, highly creative projects.

Chapter 17

I was closing the bookstore when Adrian showed up. He brought the sandwich board in with him from the sidewalk.

He didn't say anything to me. He looked annoyed. What else was new?

I didn't say anything to him.

We hadn't been in communication since the previous night, with the exception of the text I'd sent him about Cujo's newest groupie. He was the one who hadn't replied. I was the one who was annoyed at him.

With a solemn expression, he turned the lock on the front door.

I went back to what I'd been doing, counting the money for the float.

Adrian came over, watched me for a moment, then nudged me out of the way and pulled open the drawer. I'd placed a half-sucked-on cough drop right where he'd see it.

He sucked in air audibly when he saw the cough drop.

I kept a poker face. Internally, my cheerleading squad did a victory routine.

Adrian plucked the cough drop from the drawer and chucked it into the garbage.

I said nothing.

He left my side and went into the back office, where he aggressively yanked open the drawers of the filing cabinets.

I had left his precious new files exactly where he'd put them. All I had done was put my own personal touch on his system. I'd added sparkling stickers to every one of the file folders and labels.

He closed the drawers and walked out of the office without saying anything.

Next, he checked the plant pots on top of the bookshelves. I'd watered the plastic ones earlier that day. I'd watered them extra well.

Adrian shook his head at me then headed down the hallway that led to the bathroom.

I crossed my fingers, hoping he would appreciate the new decorations I'd put up in the washroom. I'd printed out posters for the rival musical group that had allegedly stolen songs from Adrian's favorite, Megasoystick.

The bathroom hallway area was very quiet.

While Adrian was taking in the brilliance of all my hard work, I brought the day's sales reports back into the office to file away for Mr. Olivier.

I placed the new report exactly where Adrian had wanted it—in the file folder with the unicorn stickers.

When I turned around, I found Adrian standing in the doorway of the tiny office, watching me.

I squared my shoulders and faced him. Now what?

He took two steps toward me, stopped, leaned down, and kissed me.

There was an energy to his kiss that hadn't been there seven years ago. Adrian Stromquist was no longer a shy, brooding teenager. He was all grown up now, and it showed in his kiss, and then in his embrace.

I pulled away from his face and said breathlessly, "Are you sure you locked the front door?"

"You saw me lock it," he said, looking more agitated than ever.

"I know, but..."

He was kissing my neck. I forgot all about the door.

It was locked, by the way. Which was a good thing, considering what happened next.

Chapter 18

In the morning, I opened the bookstore to find the lights on, the alarm off, and Adrian hunched over the computer. He was as still as a statue, his elbows on either side of the computer keyboard.

I approached cautiously. His eyes were closed. As a teenager, he used to sleep sitting up in chemistry class, but this was remarkable. He was standing and sleeping, like a horse. No. Like a giraffe.

I pulled out my phone and took some photos. He still didn't wake up. I looked around for something fun to do to him. I pulled lipstick from my purse to give him a makeover. As soon as the lipstick touched his lips, he woke up with a start.

His sudden movement made me scream.

My scream made him scream.

He blinked, recovering quickly, then asked, "Is this a dream?"

"Yes, Adrian. This whole thing is a dream."

"That explains so much." He snaked his long arms around me, pulling me into his embrace. I let him hold me a moment then pulled away before things got out of control. We had to be careful. I hadn't locked the front door behind me.

I stepped out of his reach and said curtly, "And good morning to you, Mr. Operations Manager." I looked him over. "Those are the same clothes you were wearing yesterday. Have you been here all night?"

He smirked. "After you left, I was too stunned to do much of anything."

"I do have that effect on men." I started flicking on the lights. "But you should have gone home for some sleep."

"I was working on the database until late," he said. "So I decided to stay up and have breakfast with you." He rubbed his stomach. "But now I don't feel so great."

"You're probably dehydrated," I said. "You worked up quite a sweat last night, when you were... showing me how to file alphabetically."

"It was worth the effort," he said. "By the second attempt, you were almost getting the hang of it."

"That's not what your face said last night. Your face told me that the student had surpassed the master."

He wrinkled his nose. "I'm not so sure about that. This morning, I noticed some discrepancies in your filing work." He nodded toward the office playfully. "Meet me in there so we can go over everything again."

"I don't think so." I crossed my arms. "You were sleeping at the computer like a giraffe when I walked in. I had a full night's sleep. If you tried to show me something right now, you'd be dangerously outmatched, Mr. Stromquist."

He snorted. "I could out-file you with one hand tied behind my back." He yawned.

I grabbed his arm and steered him toward the door. "Please go home. You're making me tired just looking at you."

He leaned down to kiss me. We were standing by the front door, where anyone passing by could have seen us. I gave him a quick peck then pulled away.

"Get some sleep," I said.

"The new database is up and running," he said, waving at the counter. "I had to upgrade all the drivers, but it's functional now."

"Is that why the old gal is smoking? Don't look now, but I think our antique computer system is on fire."

Adrian grinned and kept his eyes on me. "Then treat it like you do the plastic plants and water it."

"I'm not going to water the plastic plants anymore," I said. "I'm not going to do any of the stuff I did yesterday. That was a one-time-only deal."

He pouted. "I don't like it when you say stuff like that. I might have hurt feelings if I didn't know it wasn't true."

"It is true," I said. "Yesterday was a huge mistake. I shouldn't have let you boss me around with the filing system."

His eyebrows went up. "You seemed plenty eager to learn new skills last night."

"Those weren't new skills," I said coolly.

He frowned. "Are we actually talking about filing?"

I opened the front door for him. "Just go home," I said. Busy street sounds streamed in.

He said, "Call me if the new inventory system gives you any trouble."

"I can't imagine anything in this bookstore giving me more trouble than what I get from you."

He looked into my eyes. "You love the trouble I give you." He leaned down and growled near my ear, "You loved every minute of it last night."

I used both of my hands on his chest to push him away. "Get some sleep," I said. "I promise to call you if the computer blows up."

He grinned as he left.

After he was gone, I leaned against the wall next to the door and hyperventilated.

Was this my life now?

My romantic life had always been one disaster after another, but, until now, at least my job had been rock solid. Bookworm Books was my sanctuary. My happy place. The one perfectly pleasant thing that kept me from having to meditate—something I hadn't done once since leaving the makeup chair in Los Angeles.

Now the store would be downsizing and moving, which was bad enough on its own. On top of that, Adrian would be around constantly as my... operations manager? Boss? Boyfriend?

Last night had been exciting and spontaneous, a mix of old memories and new muscles—his, mostly. At last we'd finally dealt with the simmering tension. We'd joyously relived our nostalgia and gotten it out of our system. More than once.

My breathing gradually slowed down to normal.

There was no need to panic. Not really.

I'd had a full night's sleep, and then I'd come to my senses in the bright light of morning.

Adrian had been up late working, so his mind wasn't working right. As soon as he rested, he'd realize how silly it was for the two of us to be anything more than friends.

Chapter 19

At two o'clock on Tuesday, Adrian walked into the bookstore with my part-time employee, Garnet Langtree.

"Hi, Garnet," I said. "I know you want more hours now that it's the summer, but you're not scheduled to work today."

"I am now," Garnet said. "The new operations manager gave me a bunch more hours."

"Did he now?" I blinked at Adrian. "What magical budget is your paycheck going to be coming from?"

"You leave the budget worries to me," Adrian said, tapping his temple. "Near-genius IQ, remember?"

"Near-genius isn't genius," I said. "A parrot has a near-genius IQ, compared to a goldfish."

"I know," Adrian said gravely. "Parrots should not be kept in cages. They're highly intelligent creatures. The poor things require constant stimulation."

"Sounds like some people I know," I said.

Garnet narrowed his eyes and glanced back and forth between us. "You two are totally doing it," he said.

I laughed very hard. "Oh, Garnet." I shook my head and said to Adrian, "From the mouths of babes."

Adrian grinned as he walked over to Garnet and offered him a high-five. Garnet slapped his hand hard.

"Yeah, bro," he said.

I raised an eyebrow at my employee. "Really?"

Garnet shrugged.

"Let's get out of here," Adrian said to me. "This young upstart will take care of things until closing. Isn't that right, young man?" He ruffled Garnet's hair, which was a lovely shade of red and hard to resist.

Garnet laughed and play-wrestled with Adrian, which was a much more positive response than the reaction I got whenever I ruffled the kid's hair.

I reached for my purse tentatively. "Where are we going?"

"Elsewhere," Adrian said.

"Swell," I said sarcastically. "I've always wanted to go elsewhere on a Tuesday afternoon."

Adrian said to our teen employee, "Get on that computer and tell me if the new system makes sense to you. I can give you a quick tutorial while Peaches goes next door to get us some coffee and donuts for the road."

He started showing Garnet how to use the computerized inventory system, which was much easier than our previous system, which was old enough to have been forged by dwarves deep in Middle Earth.

I went next door to get donuts, for that was a task I did not have to be asked to do twice.

Donut Joe's smelled amazing, as usual. It wasn't very busy.

Rhonda packed up my order and asked, "Where's the party?"

"It's in my pants," I said. "Or it probably will be soon."

She snorted. "Figured as much. I saw Lover Boy walk by a few minutes ago."

"Rhonda, have you ever known you were going to do something you'd regret, but also know you're just going to do it anyway?"

"Almost every day," Rhonda said. "Want to talk while I take my smoke break?"

"Sure."

Rhonda gave some instructions to her coworkers then grabbed her lighter.

I left my donuts on the counter and followed Rhonda out the back door to the alley, where I picked a spot upwind of her.

She lit her cigarette. "Did I ever tell you about the time my cousin Donny paid me to make a man out of his young prep cook?"

I made the appropriate shocked expression.

"Not like that," Rhonda said. "I was just supposed to kiss him a bit." She took a long drag. "But who knows, right? One thing always leads to another."

"What are you saying? Did you sleep with the kid?"

"Nope." She shook her head and looked sad. "They found a substitute. A much younger substitute. It's hard for old gals like us to get honest work." She let out a gravelly laugh, then said, "That was a joke, Peaches. You're not old. You have a few years left on your warranty."

"Thanks," I said.

She took the longest drag I'd ever seen anyone take, plus some. Breathing out smoke, she said, "You have your fun with the fellas while they still want you. No regrets. That's what I always say."

"I already had some fun with Adrian," I said. "Last night. In the office of the bookstore." Now that Garnet knew, what was the point in being coy about it?

Rhonda punched my upper arm. "Good for you," she said.

"But he's technically my boss right now. How am I supposed to work under him if I'm also, you know, *working under him*?"

"That's his problem," Rhonda said sagely. "Besides, he won't be working with you for long. After the move, you never have to talk to him again."

"You'd think," I said. "Unfortunately, we have family connections. I'll be seeing him around at Christmas and Thanksgiving for years. Probably every year until we're dead."

Rhonda gave me a disgusted look. "You two are related? Forget what I said. Take a cold shower and get some space."

"It's not like that," I said.

"Then how is it?"

I wanted to tell Rhonda the truth but I couldn't. Sure, we had donut-seller-client confidentiality, and I didn't think she'd tell anyone about Elliot, but what if she let it slip by accident? I'd never forgive myself.

"Our moms are really good friends," I said. "That's all."

Rhonda ashed her cigarette in the dumpster. "Do your moms want you two to get together?"

Without mulling over the question, I immediately said, "Yes."

She pointed her cigarette at me. "That's your problem. You don't want to do what the moms want you to do. You're a rebel. Nobody's the boss of you, Peaches Monroe."

"You're not the first person who's mentioned that to me this week. Do you think that's what my problem is? I only want to do what I'm not supposed to do?"

She gave me a duh look.

The back door to the bookstore swung open. An irritated-looking Adrian stepped out, scowled at me, and said, "There you are. I've been waiting in here for you."

"Give me five more minutes," I said, waving him off.

He frowned but went back inside the bookstore, leaving us to our alley chat.

Rhonda raised her eyebrows at me. "He *is* a bossy one. Are you going to take that attitude from him?"

"I'm afraid it's all part of the appeal."

Rhonda pursed her lips. "You might have to spank him for being so disrespectful to you in front of your friend."

"He's a big boy. I'm not sure I could bend him over my knee."

"I'm sure you could." Rhonda laughed knowingly.

Chapter 20

It turned out that Adrian's idea of playing hooky from work on a Tuesday afternoon involved going to every liquidation center in the city, looking for a new counter. Our existing store counter had seen better days, and it was too large for the smaller space. It would stay behind for the wine shop, albeit with significant upgrades.

After hitting up every warehouse around, we found a bunch of fixtures we both liked and arranged for delivery.

The owner of the place informed us that his delivery guy was going on summer vacation, so our options were to either get the counter and shelves delivered later that night or wait two weeks.

"Tonight," Adrian said.

At the same time, I said, "Two weeks is fine."

Adrian shot me a look. "Tonight works for us," he said with authority to the owner of the liquidation center. "I'll be there myself to take delivery."

While the man did the paperwork, I asked Adrian, "What's the rush?"

"It's not rushing to get a delivery right away," he said. "It's appropriate for business. We found what we wanted, and now we're taking it."

I narrowed my eyes at him. "That does fit with your attitude in general, about other things. You find what you want, and you take it."

"That's how business works," he said, pointing to his temple. "I'm very good at business. Near-genius IQ, remember?"

"So you keep telling me. I guess I don't have a head for business."

"You have other skills," he said.

"Are you saying I'm not good at business?"

"You have *soft* skills."

I snorted. "At least I'm not a burnout, living at home and driving my mom's car."

He stared at me, his blank expression giving away nothing. "That situation is temporary."

"Everything is temporary, if you want it to be," I said.

"You may be right." He smiled and returned his attention to the transaction. He handed over the corporate credit card that Gordon Olivier had given him to make purchases for the store.

As we were preparing to leave the liquidation center, Adrian said, "Use the washroom here. We're going for a long drive, and I don't know when we'll be around another one."

"More shopping? Aren't we done yet? It was fun at first, but the novelty of digging through dirty old stained hotel furniture has really worn off. It's like one of those antiques shows but without any payoff. And what's the deal with all the lamps? Why did furniture designers make lamps so big? And for so many decades?"

"The lamps were big for a long time," he said.

"My mother got into gourd-shaped lamps for a few years, but now gourds are over, so she's all about the narrow cylinders."

Adrian waited for me to finish talking then said, "The counter delivery isn't coming for hours. It's going to be a long day for us. I figured we'd take a break and drive out to Phantom Bog. My mother said the orchids are in bloom."

"Since when are you into orchids?"

He shrugged. "It's something to do." He checked the time on his phone. "If you're not interested in a nature walk, we could get back to Bookworm by closing. After it's shut down, we could kill some time by cleaning up some of those product codes that didn't scan."

I backed toward the liquidation center's customer washroom. "The bog sounds lovely," I said. "Who doesn't love a bog?"

Adrian grinned. "I knew you'd see it my way."

Chapter 21

Phantom Bog was near the Weston Estate but not part of the estate. There were public walking trails, designated areas for visitor parking, and no signs warning away trespassers. I didn't expect to be chased out of there by drones and imaginary SWAT teams.

Adrian parked at the side of the road and let Cujo out of the car. There was one other vehicle parked there. The bog didn't see much action on a Tuesday afternoon.

The dog bounded off into the woods, wagging his tail like a puppy. When he wasn't biting me on the butt, Cujo was not nearly as terrifying as his namesake, the rabid St. Bernard in the Stephen King book.

I stopped to read a laminated sign posted by the hiking trail. "Adrian, it says there have been cougar and bear sightings in the area."

"That's normal for this time of year," he said. "Don't worry about seeing any cougars."

"Why? Are you going to protect me?"

"Because if a cougar wants to eat you, you'll never see it until it's on top of you."

I held back. "Maybe we should do this another time. There's a truck stop not far from here that makes mile-high pie to die for."

"Sounds like a great option for dinner. Tell you what. I'll take you there. My treat. But first we have to work off our donuts with a walk around the bog."

"Curse you for being practical."

Adrian propped his long leg on a rock and leaned forward. "Stretch your calves and hammies. The bog is about a half hour's walk from here. The terrain is mostly flat, but a stretch now will help prevent injuries if you stumble."

"Hammies?" I stretched lazily then began working on my hamstrings. "Do you really say hammies, or is that just for my benefit?"

"I say hammies. This is the real me, Peaches. I'm not playing a role."

"I didn't say you were playing a role."

"No, but if I'd been played for a fool like you were by Dalton Deangelo, I'd be wary of guys for a while."

"He didn't play me," I said with a snort. "I told him to take a hike. We barely dated before I ended things."

"But you only ended things because I made you read that script. I made you see the truth."

I rolled my eyes. "You had no idea what was in that script. You only wanted to read it to make fun of Dalton's project. You couldn't possibly have known ahead of time what the story was about."

"Don't be so sure about that," he said. "I know people. I have my sources. I knew immediately that he was using you for research."

"You did not."

He gave me a smug, self-satisfied look. "My cousin Lars is dating the actress who plays Harper."

"Lars? Lars Lundin? You can't believe anything that guy says. Isn't he the one who left his fiancé at the altar last summer? That guy is a grade A dirtbag."

"But he was right about the script."

I stared at Adrian while the pieces fell into place.

"That's how I knew," Adrian said.

"It's all making sense now," I said slowly. "That's why you knew so much about the story. I knew there was no way you could have read that much when we were in the kitchen." I put my hands on my hips and glared at him. "If you knew before I did, then why didn't you just tell me?"

He put his hands on his hips, mocking me with a mirror pose. "Maybe because I figured you'd react like this."

"Oh." I dropped my hands away. The anger faded fast with the posture change. "You were just trying to look out for me."

"I always have," he said. "When you started gaining all that weight in high school, I was the one who suggested you go see a doctor."

"Are you saying you knew I was pregnant?"

He looked away.

"Adrian," I said sternly. "Did you know?"

He looked down at the ground, his cheeks reddening.

"You knew," I said. "You knew, and you didn't tell me. I could have died, Adrian."

He gave me an angry look. "You think I don't know that? You think I don't think about that every day? About how the girl I loved almost died giving birth to our child?"

I took a step back and threw my hands up. "Easy now. I'm *so sorry* I didn't consider *your* feelings about how my pregnancy impacted *your* precious life, Adrian. Obviously I'm the one who's a selfish jerk. I should have been more sensitive to what *you* were going through." My voice was getting louder, and I finished at a yell. "What with how you kept on living your life exactly the same as though nothing had happened!"

Two hikers emerged from the woods and gave us wary looks. The taller man asked us, "Is everything okay here, folks?"

Adrian said to the guys, "Nature is so soothing, isn't it? We've been going through some stuff lately. I think a hike will do us some good."

The hikers both looked at me. The tall one said, "Do you want to be here, miss? Are you okay with this guy?"

I composed myself. "I'm okay with this guy," I said. "He means well. He just has a funny way of showing that he cares about someone."

The tall one put his arm around the other guy and said to him, "See? It's normal to fight sometimes. It's part of healthy communication."

The other guy pouted. "You started it," he said.

The two continued bickering between themselves as they walked down the road to their own vehicle.

Cujo emerged from the forest and barked at us.

Adrian made the dusting-off gesture with his hands. "I'm glad we cleared that up," he said.

"Wait a minute," I said. "Let's back it up a minute. You loved me?"

He blinked. "In high school." He held my gaze. "And as for the pregnancy, I didn't know. Not for sure. It was more of a strong hunch."

"But when I was constantly popping those antacids, you did tell me to see a doctor."

"I did," he said. "And you didn't go."

I looked away. "I thought about going, but I didn't want to deal with whatever was happening."

"Did you know?"

I shivered. "No. Maybe. I don't know. Maybe, on some level. Denial is pretty powerful."

"It is," he said.

Cujo came over to me and nudged me with his nose. I bent down and gave him some pets. "Ah, to be simple. Like a dog. You've got it pretty good, don't you, Cujo? Walk, eat, sleep, repeat."

"Shall we?" Adrian started toward the forest.

"I don't have hiking boots on," I said.

"Runners are fine for this trail. They've got wooden bridges over the swampy parts."

"Darn," I said. "I can't think of any more excuses to not go. I should have refused to use the washroom at the liquidation center."

Adrian smiled. "Come on. It's a perfect day to be here. There's nowhere else I'd rather be."

He held out his hand.

I was still reeling with emotional whiplash from our conversation, but I took his hand.

We'd never held hands before. We'd done a lot of research with each other when we'd been working on our screenplay, but never in public.

We walked into the woods.

I was surprised that, in spite of our height and stride differences, it was quite comfortable to walk next to Adrian Stromquist, holding his hand. Who knew?

Chapter 22

As we moved deeper into the woods, where the summer sunshine was sucked up by tree branches, Phantom Bog really earned its ominous name.

As we walked, Adrian and I didn't revisit the subject of what had happened back in high school, or how Adrian had felt about me at the time. He had said he'd loved me, though. I'd heard it with my own ears. Had he cared more about me than I had about him? I'd always been attracted to him, and fascinated by him, but I wouldn't have said I was in love with him. Could teenagers even be in love, anyway? What did kids know about grown-up feelings?

"That new counter is going to be perfect," Adrian said. "Thanks for coming with me to pick things out."

"I had fun. Thanks for taking my input."

"I figured I had to. If I got a counter you didn't like, I'd never hear the end of it."

"You are not wrong."

"I know you, Peaches. Sometimes I think I know you better than you know yourself."

We were getting dangerously close to talking about our ancient history, which would have led to another argument, so I quickly said, "What about signage?"

"That's a tricky one," he said. "Delilah's has that giant teacup. There's no way we can compete with that."

"It's a teapot," I said.

"Are you sure? Your powers of perception are not exactly impeccable."

"It's a teapot," I repeated. "Maybe we could do something three-dimensional as well. Like a book. A book would go well with a teapot."

"But a book is boring. It's just a rectangle."

"How about a stack of books?"

"Not bad," he said. "You're catching on." He let out a long, weary-sounding breath. "There's so much that needs to be done. I'm glad I'm here in the forest where I can't stare at my spreadsheets."

"You're really taking this job as operations manager seriously, aren't you?"

"Why wouldn't I?" He slowed down and looked over at me as he squeezed my hand. "It's our future that's at stake."

I got a chill down my spine. *Our future.*

"Being next to a busy diner like Delilah's is a good thing for us," he said. "We can capitalize on the weekend brunch lineups by putting some book displays on the sidewalks. Just on days when the weather is good."

"We could put out complimentary seating."

"But not too much seating," he said. "It's not a library or a community center. We don't want to attract more of those people who think money magically goes into the cash register from the sheer presence of warm, breathing bodies inside the store."

"You worked one Sunday and you already figured it all out, didn't you?"

He pointed at his temple with his free hand. "Head for business, remember?"

"People who come in just to hang out mean well. They genuinely think they're helping us out by reading the magazines for free. You have to laugh about it. Not everyone has a head for business."

"They do not," he grumbled. "What is with the old ladies who copy the recipes out of cookbooks?"

"You got some of those on Sunday? Wow. You really got the full bookstore experience."

"They're so brazen, too. One of them asked to borrow a pen!"

"Those old ladies are pretty brazen."

"They're pirates," he said. "I'm banning them from the new location."

"You can't ban old ladies, Adrian."

"I can ban recipe pirating. It's within our right."

"You're a cold man, Adrian Stromquist. Remind me not to get on your bad side."

"You wouldn't ban those grannies and their notebooks if you could?"

"I'm not a monster," I said.

We walked a bit longer, then I said, "If we're going to be setting up new rules, I would like to ban people who deliberately crack the spines of books they're not buying."

"See? I'm not the only monster here. We all have our breaking points."

"My breaking point is constantly being tested. Did you know Nisha reads the last page of books to find out the ending first?"

"She does not."

"Oh, she does."

"But she seems like such a sane, rational... oh, okay. Yeah, I can see her doing that."

"We've come to physical blows a few times over it."

He chuckled. "You and Nisha are quite the pair. I'm glad you two are still best friends. It's nice to know that no matter what changes in the world, some things stay the same, especially around here."

"A few things have changed." I squeezed his hand.

He looked down at our joined hands then up at me. "This isn't that different. It feels to me like we just picked up where we left off after graduation."

"How did Sunshine and Brittany take the news?"

"What news?"

"You didn't tell them that you and I are, you know...?"

"Exactly," he said. "I don't know what we are, so how could I tell them?"

"So, you're just going to string both of them along indefinitely?"

"We're friends," he said. "That's all."

"Hmm," I said. "Sounds to me like you're keeping a couple of spares in your back pocket in case you need something soft to land on."

"Ouch," he said. "That's a harsh thing to say about a person."

"That's literally exactly what you said to me the night of the sausage rolls. You said I was upset over Dalton, and I only wanted you to break my fall."

"Was I wrong?"

"We're human beings, Adrian. We're always falling from something. That's why they call it falling in love. Duh."

"Did you just make that up?"

"I did," I admitted. "It's pretty good, right?"

"You always had a way of joining ideas. My screenplays were so disjointed until you helped bring them together."

"Is that your subtle way of asking me to help you with your current project?"

"That's on hold until we get the store moved," he said. "But maybe we could get the old team back together, and who knows? You must have made some connections when you were in LA."

I stopped in my tracks and gave him a wary look. "Are you using me for my Hollywood connections?"

"Yes," he said. "You got me. I take no pleasure from your brilliant mind, your intoxicating presence, and your phenomenal body. Girls are icky. I'm only going through the motions so I can sell my screenplay."

"My body is phenomenal?"

He raised his eyebrows. "Do you really need me to tell you that? Wasn't your whole modeling contract a pretty clear indicator?"

I shrugged. "People have different tastes."

He put his arms around me and looked down into my eyes. "I like how *you* taste." He kissed me.

"It's my lip gloss," I said. "It's a fruit blend."

He kissed me some more, thoroughly removing the lip gloss, then pulled back, a satisfied look on his face.

"If I get chapped lips, it's on you," I said.

"Come on," he said. "We haven't even seen the bog yet."

We walked some more.

We were still holding hands when we stepped out into a clearing in the trees. In the center of the clearing, there were orange ribbons stretched between posts in the ground, marking off areas that had been recently restored. There were signs letting people know they could walk around and explore the bog as long as they kept themselves and their pets off the sensitive areas.

We didn't have to worry about Cujo, because he was more interested in the treed side of the trail.

"This is it," Adrian said. "Phantom Bog."

"It's a bog, all right."

The bog wasn't as muddy as I'd expected from the name. It didn't look much different from the surrounding trees, except the ground was lower and open. There were white and purple wildflowers dotting the sparse grass. Small birds hopped around, feeding on bugs and looking at us sideways.

Cujo trotted over and sat expectantly at our feet.

"Good dog," Adrian said. He dug into his pocket and gave Cujo a treat. The toothless old fellow gummed away happily.

"I don't see any orchids," I said. "But it's pretty out here. I can see why you like it."

"I haven't been here in ages," he said. "My mom suggested we take a trip up here."

"Oh, did she? Have you told her about us? Does she know what a maniac you are about teaching me how to file alphabetically?"

He said plainly, "I don't keep stuff from my mother."

"And she doesn't keep stuff from mine," I said. "They're probably planning our wedding right now."

He gave me a sweet smile. "Would that be so bad?"

I stared at him.

He laughed. "The look on your face! I'm just kidding, Peaches. Why would I want to mess up what we have now? This is perfect." He leaned in and stroked the side of my face. "Everything's great right now."

I said, "First the romantic bog and now the romantic talk. I'm under your spell, Adrian Stromquist. You'd better kiss me again before we start another fight."

Adrian took my comment as a command.

He planted his lips on mine.

We slowly made our way over to a log, took a seat, and continued making out.

A few items of clothing were in the process of being removed when we were interrupted by the sound of Cujo growling.

Adrian pulled his face and hands away from me.

He asked the dog, "What is it, boy?"

Cujo seemed to be growling at us.

"We're just kissing," Adrian said with a laugh. "Are you jealous?"

Cujo bared his gums and continued growling.

"So much for the romantic ambiance," I said.

Cujo kept growling, his lips curled back in a snarl. His hackles were up, the fur on his back standing in a ridge.

Adrian and I both must have had the same thought at the same time. We turned our heads in unison, looking to see what was behind us.

I saw the forest, and a black spot. Right in the middle of my field of view was the distinct absence of forest. The absence of anything.

Except it wasn't a black spot of nothingness.

It was a bear.

The bear was still at first. Then it raised its snout up, sniffing the air. I could actually hear its breaths as it sniffed.

The bear raised up slowly, standing on its back legs.

Cujo switched from growling to barking.

"Stay calm," Adrian whispered to me. "It's just a black bear. It's more scared of us than we are of it."

"Speak for yourself," I whispered back.

Cujo made his move, running past us, barking furiously. The dog stopped halfway between us and the bear.

"Cujo," Adrian said. "Get back here." He called the dog's name again, as well as some instructions in German. The dog ignored him.

The bear began bobbing from side to side in a way that was simultaneously cute and terrifying.

"We're going to calmly walk away," Adrian said to me. "Get up from the log slowly and walk backwards. Stay low."

"Aren't we supposed to make ourselves look big?"

"That's for cougars," he said.

We got up from the log and walked backwards.

Adrian kept calling for Cujo, but the dog wasn't backing down.

The bear took a few steps to the side, and Cujo attacked, lightning fast.

The bear gave the dog one swat and sent the dog flying.

Adrian stopped backing up.

The bear looked at us, looked at the dog lying in the grass, then turned and walked away, disappearing into the forest.

We waited for what felt like an eternity then ran toward the dog.

Cujo was already on his feet by the time we reached him, but he'd been hurt. That one single swipe from the bear had cut him on the shoulder pretty bad. His furry hide was pulling away, exposing muscle and things that should never be exposed.

Adrian knelt in front of the dog. His arms were limp at his sides. He didn't say or do anything. He seemed to be in shock.

Something clicked over in my head, and I realized I was feeling calm.

Perfectly calm.

It was the same feeling I'd had seven years ago, when I'd reached down and felt the top of a baby's head emerging from my body.

My brain had said, *well, this is happening.*

This situation in the woods *was* happening, and I would have to bear down—no pun intended—and do what needed to be done.

I took off my T-shirt, ripped it, and created a wrap for the dog. I tied a knot in the fabric to secure the makeshift bandage. Cujo licked my hand.

"You're going to be fine," I said gently. "You're a tough old boy, and this is just a scratch."

I got everything tied up as tight as I could. Now, how was I going to get him back to the car? He couldn't walk. He could barely stand, and he seemed to be getting weaker by the minute. His tail drooped. His eyes had lost their brightness.

"Adrian," I said. "You have to snap out of it. I don't know if I can carry him the whole way back, and I sure can't carry both of you."

Adrian, who had been frozen solid for several minutes, finally moved.

He kneeled down and scooped up the bandaged dog in his strong arms.

"I got him," he murmured. "Thanks for everything."

"No problem," I said. "Let's get him to a vet."

"A vet," Adrian said dully.

"He's going to be okay. The vet will get him a few stitches, and he'll be as good as new."

Adrian didn't say anything. He glanced around, his eyes wild-looking. "I'm a bit lost. Can you lead the way?"

"We came in this way," I said, pointing to the barely marked trail.

"Sure," Adrian said, though he didn't sound sure about anything.

I led the way, turning back periodically with encouragement for Cujo, who was still conscious, but just barely.

Chapter 23

After an unbearable wait in the waiting room, I was relieved when the veterinarian came out smiling.

"He's resting now," she said to us. "We put him out so he won't hurt himself while his body begins the repair."

"How many stitches?" Adrian asked.

"Not too many." Her voice was high and tight. She was lying.

"How do I take him home? I don't have a crate with me," Adrian said.

The vet replied, "He's going to stay overnight, Mr. Stromquist. We can keep an eye on him better than you can."

"You don't know that," Adrian said.

"This emergency is a little more serious than the last one you were here about," she said.

"It is?"

"The situation with Munchies was a clean amputation," she said. "It sounds bad, but it was a simpler surgery."

Adrian shot me a look. I didn't know who Munchies was, or why the poor thing had needed an amputation. I didn't say anything.

The veterinarian said, "Get some sleep tonight." She looked over at me. "Both of you."

Adrian said, "But—"

She cut him off. "I'll be here late, and we have cameras set up in the recovery cages for remote monitoring overnight. I'll give you access so you can watch him, too."

"He needs to go home. He needs his favorite blanket, and..." Adrian trailed off.

"Cujo will be thrilled to get home tomorrow," the vet said chirpily. "Home to hang out with Munchies."

"Right," Adrian said. "Okay. If you think that's best."

The vet made a pouty face. "The only thing he won't like is wearing the Cone of Shame."

Adrian looked stunned. "Cone of Shame?"

"It's a plastic collar," she said. "Pets aren't like humans, who can be told what's best for them. Pets need to wear a protective cone so they don't chew out their stitches after surgery."

Adrian looked at me.

"It's true," I said. "Maybe they have an extra-large one that you can wear, so Cujo doesn't have to feel the shame alone."

Adrian turned to the veterinarian and said, "Do I have to wear a cone?"

"I believe your girlfriend is joking," the vet said.

"She's not my girlfriend," Adrian said.

I heard what he said and filed it away for later. Adrian wasn't in his right mind at the moment. I couldn't take anything he said or did too seriously.

The veterinarian excused herself, then her assistant took us back to see Cujo.

Adrian walked slowly, shuffling his feet.

Cujo was in a spacious recovery cage. The German shepherd was stretched out on his side and looking comfortable enough. They'd done a good job cleaning the blood off his fur, but it was still hard to look at the wound.

We gave him some pats through the bars of the cage—more for our benefit than his, since he was crashed out on drugs—and we left.

"It's weird to leave him here," Adrian said as he started the car. "I feel like I'm forgetting something."

"You forgot to pay," I said. "Don't worry. I'll split the vet bill with you when it gets tallied up."

"No," he said dully.

"It's only fair," I said. "Cujo was protecting me just as much as he was protecting you."

Adrian stared straight ahead and said, "Firstly, I wouldn't let you. Secondly, he has a retirement fund set up for him that covers all his care." He started the car and drove in the direction of my house.

We drove without talking. The radio was on, tuned to a local station. The announcer came on and said something about Hollywood stars taking over the town. The chatter continued. I sensed something coming. Before I could change the station, the DJ uttered a certain name. Dalton Deangelo.

I pretended I hadn't heard it. Adrian either hadn't heard it or was much better at faking it than I was.

I wanted to say something to Adrian, but I couldn't think of what.

Finally, he broke the silence.

"Peaches, I just want you to know that no matter what happens, I've been blessed to get to know you better."

"What's that supposed to mean?"

"Your actor boy is back in town," he said.

"I'm not having this conversation with you now," I said. "You're still in shock from what happened to Cujo. You need some rest. We can hang out another time."

"But he's back," Adrian said. "I'm sure you'll be back in his arms as soon as he sends his butler for you."

"Will not."

"Will too."

"Jealousy doesn't suit you," I said.

"You're not denying it."

"Because there's nothing to deny. I haven't even talked to him in weeks, and you know it. When would I find the time? You've practically been on top of me since Sunday."

He shot me a dark look.

"Don't do that," I said. "Don't look at me like you hate me. It's not fair."

"I don't hate you, and I never will. You're one of the most maddening and fascinating people I've ever known, and you have a good heart, as big as the sky. You have so much to give." He frowned ahead at the road.

"Thanks," I said flatly. "I could say all those exact same things about you."

"Thanks," he replied, equally flat in tone.

We drove the rest of the way to my house in silence.

He got out and walked me to the door.

"Cute shirt," he said.

I was wearing a sweatshirt that the veterinarian's assistant had dug out of the Lost and Found. My own T-shirt had not survived its use as an emergency dog bandage.

"I'll buy you a new shirt," he said. "To replace the other one. It's my fault for taking you into the woods and ignoring the bear warning."

"Don't worry about it," I said. "Go home and put your feet up. Call me first thing tomorrow and let me know how Cujo is doing."

He smacked his forehead. "I have to take delivery of that counter tonight."

"I'll go with you," I said, turning back toward the car.

"No need," he said. "You were right, and I was wrong. I should have waited for the delivery. I was just being stupid and impulsive, as usual, not thinking about the future."

"Adrian, you couldn't have known you were going to have a medical emergency. Don't blame yourself. Although I didn't hate the sound of that one phrase you said. What was it? I was right, and you were wrong?"

"Gloating doesn't suit you," he said.

He gave me a quick kiss and then left.

Chapter 24

Wednesday, June 22nd

I know you're worried about Cujo.

Don't worry too much. He was fine. He was wagging his tail for the veterinarian early Wednesday morning, or so I was told when I phoned the clinic directly for a report.

By the time Adrian got around to calling me at the bookstore, I was already celebrating with a peanut butter glazed donut and coffee.

"Cujo will be around to attack a lot more bears," I said to Adrian on the phone.

"I hope not," he said with a groan.

"How about you? Are you feeling like yourself again today?"

He answered, sounding irritated. "What's that supposed to mean?"

"You were rocking the shocked-zombie-apocalypse look yesterday. You were basically the walking dead, and then you had to wait around at the new store location for that delivery."

"I did what I had to do," he said sullenly. "You don't have to rub it in."

"I wasn't rubbing it in. I was just checking in."

He scoffed. "I've already got one mother, and her name is Astrid."

"Awesome," I said. "Tell her you need a diaper change or a spanking."

I ended the call.

It was too early to be getting that much attitude from the same guy who'd corrected the veterinarian for referring to me as his girlfriend.

I had filed that one away, and I hadn't forgotten.

He called my cell phone again. I let it go to voicemail.

The store phone rang. It was a vintage phone, so it didn't have caller identification.

I let that go to voicemail as well.

Then I got busy with my usual store work, plus all the new tasks to prepare for the move.

I worked hard, and was ready for a break when my mother and Elliot dropped in for a visit shortly before lunch.

"Just in time," my mother said once they were in the door. She and Elliot were wearing raincoats with the hoods pulled up. "It's about to rain cats and dogs out there!"

It was the end of June, which wasn't usually a rainy time of year, but the weather had decided to make an exception that day.

My mother pulled off Elliot's yellow rain slicker. He threw himself into my legs for a hug then made a beeline for the children's section, where he flopped onto a beanbag chair and made himself comfortable.

My mother took off her rain slicker, hung it by the front door, and flicked her hair dramatically.

"You look nice," I said to her. "I may be mistaken, but I believe there's something different about you. New boots?"

"I got highlights and lowlights." She continued to fluff her golden locks. "Astrid recommended her guy. Did you know the poor woman is almost completely gray? I had no idea. She gets it touched up every three weeks like clockwork."

"She doesn't need to try so hard," I said. "More and more women are embracing the gray these days."

"So I am told."

"Astrid could pull it off. She's so tall and elegant."

"She really is," my mother said.

A customer who'd been in the store for about an hour came up to the counter to buy some books. My mother browsed around until I was finished and the customer had left. It was only the three of us in the store, so we had our privacy.

"Poor Adrian," my mother said when she returned to the counter. "I heard what happened."

"Adrian will be just fine," I said. "Poor Cujo. What an incredibly brave yet stupid dog."

"Yes, well, that's how men are," my mother said. "I'm just so glad neither of you were hurt. What were you doing up at Phantom Bog?"

"Hiking," I said. "I'm a hiker now. Don't you remember that whole thing with me all over the internet, running through the woods in my underwear?"

"Oh, Peachy. You weren't running around in your underwear again, were you?"

"Actually, I was. I had to take my T-shirt off to make a dog sling."

"Why didn't Adrian take off his shirt?"

"He's just not as good in an emergency as I am."

"I'm not surprised," she said. "We love Adrian, but—"

"Don't say it," I said. "Don't list off Adrian's flaws and then fret about whether or not you-know-who is going to catch them. I don't want to hear it."

My mother gave me a surprised look. "You two really are getting close lately, aren't you? Working together, hiking together, and what else?"

I gave her a raised-eyebrows look. "You know what else."

"Already?"

"We've known each other for years, Mom. Don't act so scandalized. Besides, isn't this what you and Astrid wanted?"

Her hands fluttered at her cheeks. "I don't know," she said. "It's all happening so fast."

"Don't get ahead of yourself," I said. "Whenever we're together, there's always a fight about something. He called this morning to let me know how Cujo was doing, and he picked a fight over absolutely nothing."

"Oh, dear."

"And yesterday, he told me he knew about you-know-what the whole time back in high school, and that's why he told me to see a doctor about my heartburn."

My mother wrinkled her nose. "He couldn't have known."

"That's what I said. But what if he did?"

"Never mind that," she said with a hand wave. "It's in the past. What's next? Is he going to move out of his parents' house? I don't think you should let him move in with you and Nisha. It's not fair to Nisha, and it's too soon. Wait until you're engaged at least before you live together."

"Nobody's getting engaged," I said. "I'm considering blocking his number and never seeing him again. I would, but we've got this whole store move coming up."

"You two always make up after your fights."

"You mean I always forgive him," I said. "Because I'm a sucker."

She stared off at the distance. "You could announce your engagement at Christmas. That would make a nice toast at dinner, don't you think? We could have Erik and Astrid over, and we could all be together. One big, happy family."

I stared at her. "Mom, when they did your hair, did they leave the chemicals on your skull for a really long time? I think they might have seeped into your brain."

She blinked at me. "They used foils," she said matter-of-factly. "That way it doesn't burn the scalp."

"Oh," I said. "That's smart."

"It's the best way," she said. "Astrid told me."

"Did you really get lowlights? I can't tell."

"You have to look underneath." She leaned over the counter and lifted up her hair.

"They did a nice job," I said. "It's very blended."

The door opened, and in walked Dalton Deangelo.

He took one look at my mother and said, "Mrs. Monroe!" He held out his arms.

My mother had always been an eager and enthusiastic hugger, but I'd never seen anything like what happened next.

She jumped three feet in the air, floated, and then soared in a ten-foot arc into Dalton Deangelo's arms. Or at least that was how it looked from where I was standing.

Chapter 25

After answering my mother's twenty-five questions, and giving Elliot a shoulder ride around the store, Dalton finally came over to talk to me in private. Sort of. My mother was over in the children's section, pretending she wasn't listening.

Outside, the sound of the cars driving along Baker Street sounded even wetter as the rain poured down dramatically.

"What brings you here today?" I asked casually. While he'd been talking to my mother and giving Elliot a shoulder ride, I'd rehearsed what I was going to say. "Escaping the rain?"

"I'm always running from something, aren't I? TV reporters, my half-sister, remote-operated security drones." The Hollywood actor grinned and paused for the laugh track. I didn't laugh.

He wiped some raindrops from his brow with one sweep of his beautiful hand. "Do you have anywhere private that I might hide?"

That sounded awfully familiar.

"The washroom is for customers only," I said.

He strode over to a display table. "I'm a customer. I'm buying this." He picked up a book at random without looking and brought it to the counter.

He was attempting to recreate the day we'd met. Not the way I would have gone, but I wasn't a high-paid Hollywood actor.

"Excellent choice," I said. "It's a perfect follow-up to the book you bought last time. How did those kegel exercises work out for you, by the way?"

"Not the way I expected."

I tried to avoid looking at him, but his famous features pulled me in. His face looked the way I'd left it—perfect, from his defined jaw and prominent cheekbones to those expressive, dark-lashed eyes. His black hair was damp and shiny from the rain. The planes of his face caught the store's lighting as though the fixtures had been set up exclusively for him.

"Why are you really here?" I asked.

"A person has to be somewhere. It's physics."

"Wouldn't you rather be at a fancy treatment facility in Malibu? I hear riding horses on the beach is lovely this time of year."

"You know about that?" He gave me a wary look. "Who told you? Was it the dark-haired, good-looking kid who works here?"

"He has a name," I said. "Garnet Langtree."

"I need to speak to that young man and set him straight. It wasn't my idea that Jade cancelled her trip home. I told her to see her family, not me."

"Are you two back together? You and Jade?"

He shook his head. "No. We're barely friends. She was just looking for drama."

"She would have hit the jackpot with you," I said.

He didn't say anything.

The bookstore was very still and quiet around us. My mother was quietly reading Elliot a book while sneaking peeks at us. There were no signs of any customers on the sidewalk out front. The sudden downpour would keep customers away for a few hours.

Dalton leaned forward, resting his elbows on the counter, and spoke softly. "Tell me how to make things right between us."

"Get a time machine. Go back in time. And stick your head up your own butt."

He pulled back, blinking. "Wow. I thought that was going to go a different way, like that I should go back in time and give you a copy of that script right after we met."

"That would also have sufficed."

"I wanted to," he said. "But it felt too soon, and then... it felt too late." He blinked. "After what happened in the Airstream."

"You used me," I said. "I was nothing but research for you. You were doing that thing where actors live the life of the character they're playing. I was never even with you, Dalton. I was with *David*."

"Perhaps you were," he said coolly. "Now that you've experienced David, would you like to give Dalton a shot?"

"A shot?" I raised my fists. "Where does he want it? I can give him a double."

He glanced over at my mother and asked her, "Is your daughter always like this?"

"I'm so sorry," my mother said, jumping up and coming to join us. "She takes after her father. Peter Monroe looks like a regular man, but he is very eccentric. I tried to throw out a recliner, and he insisted on retrieving it from the curb and hauling it up to the attic. Along with a mini-fridge. But there's no bathroom up there, so now he's got a bucket, and —"

I clamped my hand over her mouth just in time. "Please excuse my mother," I said. "My father is eccentric, but he's also romantic. He buys her a new pillow every anniversary. You should see their bed. It's covered in decorative pillows. Every night, they spend ten minutes removing all the pillows, just to have to put them back the next morning."

Dalton gave us both a surprised look. "That does sound very romantic."

I dropped my hand from my mother's mouth.

She immediately blurted out, confession style, "I had relations with your father, Jocko Ranger."

I clamped my hand over her mouth again. "She's joking. What a kidder. She's a big fan of his movies, and has a wild imagination."

Dalton narrowed his emerald-green eyes at us. "If what she said isn't true, she's quite the actor," he said.

I slowly lowered my hand.

My mother said. "It's true. I met Jocko before you were born." She kept her voice low so Elliot wouldn't hear. "He seduced me in twenty minutes flat. I was the one who did the art restoration after his wife slashed the paintings."

Dalton turned to me. "Is that true?"

I nodded. "She told me about it before the day we went to the West Estate and you told me what happened between Jocko and your mother. My mom never told me who the actor was, but when I heard your story, I figured it out."

My mother patted me on the shoulder. "Our Peachy is very clever sometimes. Did you know that's her middle name? Petra Luanne Clever Monroe. Clever is an old family name."

"Interesting," Dalton said. "As for Jocko, did you and he...?"

"No babies," my mother said. "Which is surprising, considering how many times we—"

My hand was getting very good at cutting her off as needed.

Dalton tilted his head and looked from my mother to me and back again.

"Our lives are entwined," he said. "It was no coincidence I came running into this particular bookstore. It must have been fate."

Lightning flashed outside, followed by thunder, both of which made us all jump.

Dalton pointed to the window and said, "This is why production on *Waterfall* was cancelled today. Fate is funny."

"Sometimes it rains in June," I said. "I wouldn't say it was an act of divinity that brought you here today."

"You wouldn't say that," he said, his emerald eyes twinkling. "You don't believe in such things."

Elliot came up to us and announced that he had read all of the new books and wanted to go to the toy store.

Dalton asked him, "What toy store? Is there one nearby?"

"Up the street," Elliot said. "You should come with us. They have everything."

"Maybe I will," Dalton said. "I need to pick up some gifts for the crew members to apologize for messing up their summer schedule. I could get them some cool toys, or games, or puzzles."

"Okay," Elliot said, and he started pulling on his little yellow rain slicker.

Dalton smiled at me and said, "Good to see you looking so well, Peaches. Whatever you've been doing these past few weeks, keep it up. Your cheeks are rosy."

Then Dalton prepared to head out with my mother and Elliot. To go shopping at the toy store.

We didn't know it at the time, but someone at the toy store would take photos of them, which would end up on the internet and lead to all sorts of trouble.

That day, though, we couldn't have known the future. Nobody does.

I gave Elliot a kiss goodbye, my mother a hug, and Dalton a handshake.

"Have fun at the toy store," I said.

Chapter 26

Sunday, June 26th

Four days after my mother went toy shopping with Dalton Deangelo, she was still raving about the experience.

The photos of the three of them in a toy store had started showing up online, but I hadn't seen or heard about those yet.

On Sunday afternoon, my mother brought Elliot to my house so he and I could spend some quality time together while she went to the day spa with Astrid Stromquist.

She wouldn't be meeting Astrid for half an hour, so we were having coffee in the living room. Nisha was out with Sunshine and Brittany at brunch. I was glad to have the excuse to not be at brunch because the two girls who were chasing after Adrian didn't know yet that he and I were romantically entangled, and I didn't feel right being around them and not saying anything. It was Adrian's job to put on his big-boy pants and tell the girls to back off.

I refilled my mother's coffee as she went on and on about Dalton in the toy store.

When she stopped to take a sip, I diplomatically said, "I'm glad you both had fun with him."

"It was more than fun," my mother said.

I shook my finger at her. "Naughty girl. Pick on a movie star your own age."

She gave me an appropriately scandalized look. "Peachy."

"Well? You're the one who keeps gushing about him. I didn't even bring up his name."

"He's a nice boy," she said.

"Because he threw some cash around? It doesn't take much to impress you, huh?"

She gave me a dirty look. "I know he's wealthy, but not all wealthy people are generous. He didn't have to buy Elliot all this stuff."

We both looked over at the Christmas-sized haul of new toys Elliot had brought with him to my place.

Elliot was sprawled upside down on the living room's comfy chair, playing with a supposedly educational toy that looked way more fun than any of the educational toys I'd had growing up.

"It was nice of Dalton to buy all this stuff for Elliot," I said. "I'm glad he's doing a few things to atone for his previous bad behavior. Who knows? I might be able to forgive him on some superficial level. I may be able to stomach watching his series when the new season starts airing."

My mother looked me in the eyes. "It's not Elliot's heart he's after, Peachy."

I rolled my eyes. "Mom, you need to pick a team. First you want me with Dalton, then Adrian, then Dalton again. You need to make up your mind."

"Why should I have to choose? Besides, would it make any difference?"

"Probably not," I admitted.

"It was different for me," she said, gazing off into the distance. "I didn't have to choose between Jocko and your father. They were years apart."

"Plus you would have chosen Dad," I said.

She didn't answer.

"Mom."

She continued to not answer.

"Your silence to that question is not what a daughter wants to hear," I said.

"I'm just being honest. You know I love your father, but if I'd had to choose between them, I don't know what I would have done." She smiled and touched her cheek. "It's quite something to be with a handsome actor."

"It is," I said. "It's also quite something to be with a broke-but-handsome operations manager who lives with his parents. Not in the same way, obviously, but it's quite something."

"Your father was broke when we met," she said, nodding. "It was a good thing I had my nest egg for buying the house."

I shuddered. "Poor Dad. Living in the house that you bought with your..." I pointed to the area below her waist.

She giggled. "Don't forget these." She waved at her chest.

We both looked over to make sure Elliot wasn't listening. He was engrossed in his educational toy, shooting alien space ships by correctly spelling words.

My mother said, "Back when I was up to my elbows in diapers, I often wondered about the road not taken, and what might have been." She glanced over at Elliot. "Both times," she said. "I was just getting back to my career when it all happened."

"I know," I said guiltily. "I remember. You'd just gotten that new job, and you had to put it all on hold."

She leaned forward and patted my knee. "Which was the right decision," she said. "I have no regrets. I don't regret anything. But I do occasionally have these daydreams, where I imagine a different life. If parallel universes are real, then there must be another Veronica Monroe out there who's living a very different life."

"Your last name wouldn't be Monroe," I said.

"Hmm."

"You'd better not be divorced from Dad in any of these parallel universe scenarios," I said. "I hope you had the decency to take the last name of whatever good-looking, smooth-talking man took twenty minutes or less to get you—"

She shot me a warning look.

"To the altar," I finished.

She sipped her coffee then checked the time. "Well, whatever will be will be. I should get going. Astrid is always so punctual. She must do it to make me look bad."

"I'm sure that's the only reason," I said with a sniff. "Not because, unlike some people, she can correctly estimate the time it takes to get from one place to another."

My mother got up and shot me a look. "Now you're sounding just like your father." She went over to Elliot and kissed him on the head. "Be good for Peachy," she said.

He grunted without looking up from the screen.

She pointed at me. "He'd better not be in that chair when I come back later. You need to get him outside for a few minutes or he won't sleep tonight."

"I will. Adrian's coming over with Cujo, and we're going to the park."

Her posture stiffened. "Just the three of you?"

"Four, if you include the dog. Five, if Nisha gets back from brunch in time."

"You should wait for Nisha," she said.

I narrowed my eyes at her. "Why?"

She blinked rapidly. "Because."

"Because why?"

"Trust me. Bring Nisha with you. Make it a group thing. That'll be nice. We can discuss this another time."

"Oh, we will."

She gave me a hug goodbye, and then she left.

The instant my mother was out of hearing range, Elliot dropped his educational toy and asked for a cookie.

"You just had lunch," I said.

"I won't tell," he said.

"We don't have any cookies," I said, which was a lie. "We don't keep them in the house."

"I'm not a little kid anymore," he said. "You don't have to lie to me about everything."

I put my hands on my hips. "What do I lie about?"

"Lots of things. I know your TV works, and you just say it's broken because you don't want me to watch it. And I know you always have cookies."

"Anything else?"

"I know it doesn't wreck the bed when you jump on it. I jumped on my bed plenty when nobody was watching, and nothing bad happened."

"It's true," I said with a sigh. "The whole bed-jumping-ruins-beds narrative is a massive conspiracy that we adults perpetuate just to prepare the younger generation's minds for future indoctrinations into even less plausible concepts."

"You're weird, Pee-Pee." He jumped off the chair. "I know where Nisha keeps the good cookies with the marshmallows."

"The *what*? Why don't I know about these marshmallow cookies?"

"I'll show you."

I followed him into the kitchen. Sure enough, he knew about a secret stash that even I, a rent payer, didn't know about.

We were digging into the forbidden cookies when Adrian tapped on the back door.

"It's open," I yelled out.

He let himself in. He was dressed for warm weather, wearing one of his old Megasoystick T-shirts with a pair of cargo shorts and leather sandals. I'd never seen him in sandals before. He had really long toes.

"Hi," Adrian said to Elliot. "I see your big sister is teaching you about the food groups."

"It's not easy being a role model," I said.

Adrian went to ruffle Elliot's hair but seemingly changed his mind and put his hands in his pockets. He shot me an awkward, embarrassed look.

That was when I realized what my mother had been hinting about, and why she had wanted us to wait for Nisha before going to the park.

Adrian and I had never been alone with Elliot, not even when he was a baby. Then Adrian had been out of the city for five years and hadn't seen the kid much, let alone without his parents and the rest of the Monroes present.

That afternoon, inside the same kitchen where so much had already gone down that summer, was the first time the three of us had been together without anyone else around.

It was funny that, not ten minutes earlier, my mother had talked about other imagined versions of her life, and how things might have been.

I was looking right at one of my parallel lives.

Me, Adrian, and Elliot. A happy little family, the way things might have been.

Judging by the look on Adrian's face, he felt it, too.

Chapter 27

Nisha wasn't back yet when Adrian and I took Elliot to the park.

The kid didn't want to leave his new toys behind, so I let him bring one toy of his choice. He chose one of the tractors. It had a working scoop that he could use for playing in the sandbox.

Adrian played in the sandbox with him for a while, then came over to sit with me on a bench. Cujo flopped down at our feet like a good boy.

We quietly watched the kids playing.

The sun was blazing hot, but there was a slight breeze that made it perfect.

We could hear what Elliot was saying to the other kids. He was a loud kid.

Elliot proudly told everyone on the playground about how a man named Uncle Dalton had bought him the tractor.

I sensed a change in Adrian's energy. He'd heard it, too.

I turned to Adrian and explained, "Dalton came by the store on Sunday. He went with my mom and Elliot to the toy store."

Adrian stared straight ahead, his gaze fixed on some older kids who were making a sand castle.

"I know," he said. "I saw the photos on the internet."

"Of Dalton and my mom?"

"Yes."

"I had no idea. I'll have to tell her. She'll be thrilled. Talk about perfect timing. She just got her hair done."

Adrian didn't comment on my mother's hair. He said, "That loser can't go anywhere without everyone making a fuss. I don't know what the big deal is.

He's not that great. His acting is terrible. Whenever the writers on his TV show give him good lines, he mangles them while chewing the scenery."

"Oh, good," I said sarcastically. "I'm glad you're being super mature about the whole situation. Here I was worried you'd be jealous or something."

Adrian whipped his head around and frowned at me. "You can't let anything go, can you?"

"You can't just relax and enjoy a nice outing at the playground, can you?"

He went back to pouting. "I've got a lot of other things I should be doing right now."

"Is this what you were like when you were working in real estate? I have a feeling I might know why you burned out so spectacularly, and why there was no girlfriend there to help you through it."

He dropped his head forward as though my words had been a physical blow. He continued leaning forward until he was folded over his legs, stretching his long arms down to hug Cujo, who was resting on the ground at Adrian's feet. Cujo was still wearing the Cone of Shame, but his wounds were healing without any sign of infection. So that was one thing that was going right for us.

"I know she's a meanie," Adrian said, pretending to be having a conversation with the German shepherd. "That's just her sense of humor. It runs in her family, but it does skip a generation sometimes. That's why Aunt Veronica is such a nice lady, even though she looks almost the same as Peaches."

"Don't even try to turn him against me," I said. "He's very smart. He can tell good people from bad, and he knows when you're lying. Isn't that right, Cujo?"

Cujo whipped his head toward me at the sound of his voice, smacking Adrian in the chin with the plastic cone.

"Good boy," I said. "Cujo is the best boy ever."

Adrian sat up again, rubbing his chin.

"Don't apologize," he said to me sourly.

"I wasn't going to."

He sighed. "But I did have a smack in the face coming to me. I shouldn't have been trash-talking my rival."

"He's not your rival," I said. "You're not playing a game with him, and I'm not some sort of prize. I mean, I am a prize, but not like that."

Adrian scowled.

I said, "So what if he came by the bookstore one time, then went on an errand with my mom and threw some cash around? That's what rich people do. It doesn't change how I feel about him. I'm not going to fall for his corny lines again."

"I wish I could believe that."

We sat in silence for a moment, then I said, "Adrian, have you ever heard of a self-fulfilling prophecy? The more you talk up me and Dalton, the more I start to think maybe there's something to it."

Adrian pretended to zip his lips.

"That's better," I said.

The mom of another kid who was playing in the sand with Elliot came over to us, smiling. She stopped and nervously held back, giving Cujo a wary look.

She asked, "Is your dog friendly?"

"As long as you're not running away like a perp," I said.

Adrian said, "He's toothless. His breath is worse than his bite." He shot me a look. "Contrary to some rumors, he is a very friendly dog when he's not on duty."

The woman came up and kneeled to let Cujo sniff her hand. She was eye level with us.

"You must be Elliot's parents," she said. "He's just the spitting image of both of you. What a remarkable child!"

Adrian didn't say anything.

Normally, I would have told the woman he wasn't mine, and that I was just the big sister. That sunny Sunday afternoon, though, I didn't bother correcting her. I had already been emotionally taxed by Adrian, plus it was getting hot in the park, and I was starting to melt.

"Thanks," I said.

"He *is* remarkable," Adrian said, his face lighting up.

"I'm a casting agent," she said. "You must be so proud of your son. He's handsome, intelligent, and so well mannered. How old is he?"

Adrian's chest swelled. "He's only seven," he said. "His name is Elliot. It's an old family name."

"It's a beautiful name," the woman said. "We're always looking for remarkable children like Elliot. Perhaps you'd like to bring Elliot to our next open call at my office? He could be a future star."

Adrian replied, "I wouldn't want him to get distracted from his studies."

"We can work around Elliot's academic priorities," she said.

Adrian nodded. "I'll discuss it with his mother."

The woman pulled a card from her purse and handed it to Adrian.

She told us her name and shook both of our hands. Then she collected her child from the playground and left.

After she was gone, I said to Adrian, "That was an interesting reaction on your part."

He shrugged. "It was harmless. We'll never see that woman again. I'm sure it's just one of those scams where they want to sell you a bunch of photography services. Proud parents are huge suckers."

"Is that what you are?"

He snorted. "I'm not a huge sucker. I don't even want this card." He tossed it into the trash bin next to the bench.

"I meant the other thing. Are you a proud parent?"

He shifted, visibly uncomfortable. "I wouldn't say that. I know your family thinks of me as nothing but a genetic donor with questionable traits that I may have passed on to Elliot. I see how your mom and dad analyze every single thing I say or do, looking for flaws."

"You're more than just a genetic donor," I said with a snort. "You're also a giant pain in the—"

A female voice behind us exclaimed, "Oh, oh, oh!"

We both turned on the bench to see Nisha, my roommate and best friend, pointing at us. I had sent her a text message to meet us at the park, and she had come over. I hadn't heard her approaching, and she must have heard us discussing genetic donors. I'd kept Elliot's birth a secret from her this whole time, for seven long years. Judging by the look on her face, the cat was now out of the bag.

I tentatively asked her, "How much of our conversation did you hear?"

Nisha jumped up and down, holding one hand over her mouth while she pointed between us and said, "Oh, oh, oh!"

Adrian rolled his eyes. "Nisha, you don't have to act like you just found out. I'm sure Peaches told you years ago."

Nisha continued pointing. She stopped speaking.

I said to Adrian, "She didn't know."

He pulled his head back. "Really? If I'd ever had a best friend, I would have told them for sure."

Nisha went back to saying, "Oh, oh, oh!"

Cujo jumped up and started circling and sniffing, alerted to the fact that something was happening.

Chapter 28

Nisha was in shock after discovering Elliot's origins. For several minutes, she was unable to formulate normal sentences.

Cujo, however, really stepped up. The German shepherd licked her hand and helped her calm down.

"What a good boy," I said, petting his non-injured side. "Maybe you'll get your Cone of Shame off soon."

"He is a good boy," Adrian said. "Maybe he won't be retired much longer. It looks like he's got a future as an emotional support animal."

Elliot came running over to hug Nisha. She hugged him then stared at him like he was an alien.

Being seven, though, Elliot didn't notice. He grabbed Cujo's tail and pretended to be winding up the dog.

Cujo gave me a look as if to say, *First the Cone of Shame, and now I'm a wind-up dog?*

"Life's like that," I said to the dog. "One minute you're a respectable member of law enforcement, and then you're a cuddle toy."

The dog's ears perked up. He knew the word *toy*. He was a smart dog.

Elliot continued winding up the dog's tail.

Nisha continued to stare at Elliot as though he'd just stepped off a spaceship.

Adrian shoved his hands in his pockets. "Well, if it's all the same to you guys, I'll just head home from here."

"You don't want to stay for dinner?" I asked. "Nisha's making prawns vindaloo."

"Uhh," he said. "That's the spicy one?" He patted his stomach. "I'll pass."

"Your loss," I said.

He picked up Cujo's leash, said goodbye to everyone, and left the park.

Elliot looked up at me sweetly. "Can I watch your TV, Pee-Pee?"

"I don't know. Can you?"

His adorable face scrunched up. "May I watch your TV?"

"Sure," I said. "You're lucky. We just got it fixed."

Elliot turned and yelled another goodbye at Adrian and Cujo. They turned around, and Adrian had the dog wave goodbye.

We got back to the house, where we settled on watching an educational show on one of the children's channels.

My mother came to pick up Elliot, I took her out to the back yard for some privacy, and I let her know that the proverbial cat was out of the bag. She seemed surprised that Nisha hadn't known already.

"Why does everyone assume that?" I asked.

The sun was beating down on the back yard, and I was sweating.

"It's because you two are so close," my mother said. She gave me a big hug. "Don't worry about it, Peachy. I'm glad your best friend knows." She pulled away and looked at me. "How did it go with Adrian?"

"You were right," I said. "I should have waited for Nisha before we went to the park. It was eerie. And then, a woman at the park thought we were his parents." I wiped the sweat from my forehead. "And Adrian didn't correct her."

My mother frowned. "Oh, dear. I don't like the sound of that. It could get very confusing for Elliot." She tilted her head. "Or maybe not. He's almost eight, and he's very mature for his age. I suppose it might be time for him to know."

"Stick to the plan," I said. "We'll tell him when he's twelve. That's what we all agreed to."

"That's one nice thing about you dating Adrian. At least he already knows."

"True," I said.

She hugged me again, and then we went back into the house.

My mother collected Elliot and all of his toys, and they left.

Once Nisha and I were alone, I covered all the main points.

No, I hadn't known I was pregnant.

Yes, I did give birth to him in the bathtub at home, alone.

No, Adrian and his parents hadn't objected to my parents raising Elliot as their own.

Yes, my mother's friends bought the lie that she was the one who hadn't known she was pregnant. It helped that in the days following his arrival, she'd been too busy and stressed to eat, so she'd dropped enough weight to sell the story when she did see her friends after a few weeks.

After answering all those questions and more, I was dying to talk about something else—anything else—but she wasn't ready to move on.

An hour after my mother had left, Nisha was peeling the prawns for her vindaloo curry sauce while I grated the zucchini to make a noodle facsimile for our low-carb dinner. To offset my occasional indulgences, such as raiding Nisha's secret marshmallow cookie stash, I did have *some* sensible meals.

Nisha said, "I always knew there was something unusual going on between you and Adrian. The way you guys fought with each other but couldn't stay away from each other—it was more than the usual teen drama." She pointed at my bowl of zucchini noodles. "You need to put those in a strainer, or they'll be too watery."

I transferred the noodles to a strainer and asked, "Are you mad?"

She blinked at me. "I'll be mad if you make my curry watery."

I squeezed the vegetable noodles to speed the draining process.

"If I'm being perfectly honest, I'm a bit upset," she said. "I'm upset that I wasn't able to be more supportive of you when you needed it."

"You were fifteen," I said. "You had your own stuff going on. That was around the time your parents were threatening to go all traditional and hire a matchmaker to arrange a marriage for you."

She shuddered. "I'd be married with three kids by now, if it were up to them."

"Do you ever think about it sometimes? What your life would be like if you were a mom by now?"

"Noah wants kids," she said.

I gasped. "Nisha, you're not...?"

She shook her head. "Nope."

"Then why are we talking about Noah? I thought you were done with him."

She kept her dark-brown eyes focused on the prawns she was peeling. "I was late getting to meet you guys at the park today because I bumped into Noah."

"Where? At Pancake International?"

She shot me a guilty look. "At his house."

"Wow," I said. "Talk about a coincidence."

"I've been seeing him on occasion," she said. "I'm sorry I didn't tell you sooner."

"Why are you telling me now? Do you need me to stage an intervention? Should I start a fund to send you to a horse ranch in Malibu for detox treatment?"

She sniffed. "I'm only telling you because I don't want us to have any more secrets from each other."

"You know my big secret now, so we're even." I left the noodles to drain and washed my hands. "But, since we're airing out all the dirty laundry, Elliot found your marshmallow cookie stash today. We ate them all before we went to the park."

She looked at me. "Fair enough. I also have something to confess. That wasn't a dried-up baby carrot you found in your bed. It was part of a spell."

I pointed at her. "Witch! You're an amateur witch."

"You knew that about me. It's not news."

"I knew that wrinkled little thing wasn't a carrot. What other witchcraft have you been casting on me?"

She pressed her lips together. She looked extremely guilty.

"Wait," I said. "Back it up. What was the dried-up baby carrot thing for?"

She bit her lower lip. "It was a love spell."

I nodded slowly. "So, this is all your fault," I said. "Too bad you screwed it up. You must have messed up the spell. Now I've got two guys in my life who are only half right for me. Two halves make a whole in math, but it doesn't add up that way in life."

"I thought you were over Dalton?"

"I've been thinking about him ever since he popped into the bookstore to say hi."

"I thought things were good with Adrian?"

"We fight a lot."

She kept peeling prawns. After a moment, she said, "I didn't screw up the love spell. Not that magic is real, but I did it right."

"When did you cast this spell? Not that I believe in any of that nonsense, but I'm curious."

"The day before Tina's wedding," she said. "I figured there'd be some single guys around, and weddings are so romantic, plus you were moping around about not having a date."

"I was related to most of the guys at that wedding," I said. "You're lucky Dalton came running into the bookstore that day, or you and I would be having a very uncomfortable conversation about me and one of my second cousins."

"I know," she said. "I shouldn't have meddled."

She started throwing the whole spices into a frying pan to toast them. The whole kitchen filled with the scent of spice.

I sat at the table a moment, mulling over what she'd told me.

"Nisha," I said slowly.

"Yes?" She had her back to me.

"Did you cast a love spell on Noah?"

"You can't cast a love spell on yourself," she said. "With this one, it needs to be someone else who casts it."

"Nisha, did you have one of your Wiccan friends cast a spell for you and Noah?"

She shook the spices in the pan. "Oh, Peaches. Everyone knows magic isn't real. There's no such thing as magic or spells. The whole idea is not that different from traditional Cognitive Behavioral Therapy. It's just a means to redirect your thinking patterns in a more optimistic, beneficial way."

"You *did* have another witch cast a love spell for you and Noah," I said.

"I... redirected my thinking patterns," she said. "I can now clearly see that there might be a future for me and Noah."

"Until he cheats on you with a tiny blond yogi with a flat chest," I said. "Then what? Will you have your friend cast another spell to make you blind to what's in front of your face?"

She gave me a dirty look. "Sure," she said flatly. "Maybe you can give me some of whatever you've been using lately."

"Ouch."

"Adrian isn't just half-good, and neither is Dalton. They're human beings. Human beings aren't perfect. You have to take the bad with the good. The truth is, you could be happy with either one of them, if you could stop flying off the handle every time one of them slips up a little. You may not know this, Peaches Monroe, but I live with you, and I have observed that you're not exactly perfect."

"Point taken." I threw up my hands. "Go ahead and date Noah. You're a big girl. I'm not the boss of you. Maybe he's not as bad as my impression of him. What would I know?"

She pouted. "Are we fighting?"

"We're clearing the air," I said.

"I don't like it."

"Me, neither," I said.

"I think I am feeling some anger at you over not telling me about you and Adrian and Elliot. I know that's petty of me, because it was a private family matter, but I can't help how I feel. It was an enormous part of your life that you had to keep secret from me. I don't know how you did it. I couldn't have kept something like that from you."

"Maybe *I'm* angry you didn't figure it out on your own and save me the trouble of having to lie about it for all these years."

She frowned. "Are you? Are you angry at me?"

I held up my hand, my thumb and forefinger a quarter inch apart. "Maybe this much," I said.

"That's about how much I'm angry at you."

"Then we're even," I said. "Don't burn the spices."

She flashed her eyes at me playfully. "How dare you! Telling me how to toast spices?"

"They're smoking," I said.

"Oh." She pulled the pan off the element.

Chapter 29

According to Adrian's big plan, Monday was the last day Bookworm Books would be open regular hours. We would be closing at two o'clock that day to take inventory and begin the process of running a clearance sale plus moving.

In the book business, most of the product was returnable to the publishers. To cut our inventory by half, we wouldn't need to do any steep discounts to get rid of the excess. Not with the books, anyway. We would run a clearance sale on the non-book items, such as candles, fridge magnets, and other collectibles.

I was chatting with our delivery guy about our plans when Sunshine and Brittany, my brunette and blond friends, stopped into the bookstore.

As the delivery guy walked out, Brittany stared after him and asked, "Who was that?"

"Never mind that one," I said. "He's married. Or at least I think he is. He wears a wedding band."

"Oh." She wrinkled her nose. "The good ones are always taken."

"It might be a decoy ring to keep the girls from mobbing him," I said. "He is quite easy on the eyes."

Sunshine didn't say anything. She did give me a knowing look, as though I might be lying to them so I could keep the delivery guy all to myself.

The girls came around the counter to fawn over Cujo.

Adrian would be busy all morning doing some painting at the new location. He didn't need the assistance of a dog wagging his bushy tail against the freshly painted walls—go figure—so I was babysitting the German shepherd.

They both kneeled down and petted the dog.

"What are you both doing here on a Monday?" I asked. "Do you ever work?"

"I'm only part-time at the community center," Brittany said.

"I make my own schedule," Sunshine said.

I said to Sunshine, "I thought you did deliveries for your uncle's art gallery. Doesn't that mean you're sort of on-call?"

She gave me a sour look. "Yeah. Among other things. I'm also working on some new songs."

Brittany said, "We missed you at brunch yesterday, Peaches. You should have been there. They had a malfunction with the chocolate fountain and it sprayed chocolate across the table. It was the funniest thing."

"I'm sorry I missed that," I said.

Sunshine narrowed her dark eyes at me while she stroked Cujo's ears. "What were you doing yesterday? The bookstore was closed."

"Family stuff," I said. "My little brother came over, and we went to the park."

"Who'd you go with?"

I sensed she already knew. "Adrian," I said.

"Thought so," Sunshine said.

Then she went back to petting Cujo.

Brittany jerked her head up. "What? You were hanging out with Adrian yesterday?"

"Yes," I said. "He came by the house, and he tagged along when I took my little brother to the park."

She blinked rapidly. "Why?"

"For something to do," I said. "Has Adrian not told you two that he and I have been... hanging out sometimes?"

Brittany gave me a confused look. "For work stuff, right?"

Sunshine elbowed Brittany. "Don't be stupid. Adrian's in love with Peaches, and he's just stringing us along as backups." She looked up at me. "Isn't that right?"

I swallowed. "That is not an unreasonable theory, given the circumstances, but I wouldn't say he's in love with me. We're just friends."

Sunshine said, "The kind of friends who...?" She raised her eyebrows. There were customers browsing in the store, so she didn't finish her sentence.

"Yes," I said. "That's a fairly recent development."

"Except I'm guessing it isn't that recent at all," Sunshine said, glaring at me.

"Not that it's any of your business, but that started a week ago," I said. "I'd call that *recent*."

"That's not how I see it," Sunshine said.

I shrugged. "Well, it sounds like you're the expert, so why don't you tell me?"

"It's been going on for about eight years," she said. "Is that about right, Peaches?"

Brittany said, "Huh?"

I turned to the computer. "You know what? I've got a lot of work to do. If you two want to spend time with Cujo, take him out for a walk. You can take the cone off as long as you're watching to make sure he doesn't bite the stitches. He enjoys the dog fountain at the dog park. You'll make his morning if you take him there."

Brittany said, "I don't understand what's happening. Are Adrian and Peaches together?"

"Yes," Sunshine said.

"No," I said. "Not officially. Listen, I was going to tell you guys, but Adrian told me he was going to."

Sunshine tilted her head back. "Adrian likes keeping all his options open."

"So it would seem," I said.

She asked, "Are they? Are his options open?"

Something in me snapped. Adrian hadn't told the girls because he hadn't wanted to. He enjoyed having them chase after him. What kind of a guy did that? A bad one.

I couldn't believe I'd been so stupid to have fallen for Adrian and his smug, know-it-all face. He'd been using me. He was as bad as Dalton.

Sunshine stared at me, waiting for a response.

"Adrian can do whatever he wants," I said, feeling calm thanks to my sudden decision. "He can date all three of us, if that's what he wants."

"Good," Sunshine said. "Because that's what he's been doing."

Brittany's cheeks flushed. "What? You know?"

"I'm not blind," Sunshine said to Brittany. "I know we agreed to our ground rules, but what's that saying? No battle plan survives contact with the enemy."

Brittany pressed both hands to her face. "I'm so weak."

Sunshine shrugged. "At least it's all out in the open." She looked at me. "Right, Peaches?"

I reeled from the second shock of the morning. Not only was he stringing the other two members of the Quad Squad along, but he'd been physical with them. He'd crossed a line.

Sunshine was waiting for my reaction.

I crossed my arms. "Yup," I said coolly. "It's all out in the open now. Just out of curiosity, what were the ground rules?"

Sunshine said, "About what you'd expect. Has he broken the rules with you?"

I glanced back at the office. "Without knowing the specifics, I'd say probably."

"He needs to decide," Brittany said, pouting. "It's not fair, what he's doing to the Quad Squad. He's going to break us up."

"You're right," Sunshine said. "It's not fair. We should all dump him."

Brittany looked away.

I said, "You two can do whatever you want. If he's been stringing all three of us along, then I'm done with him. All we do is fight, anyway."

Brittany gave me a stunned look. "You do? What would you fight about? He's perfect."

"Mah," I said. "Mr. Perfect is all yours."

Sunshine frowned.

"Or yours," I said to her. "I'm out, ladies. You have my word. Adrian Stromquist is all yours. You can toss a coin, or you can cut him in half down the middle. I don't care because it's not any of my business. Not anymore."

Brittany said, "I do like my odds better when there's only two of us."

Sunshine said to her, "Two of us, *that we know of.* Maybe there are more."

I had to laugh. "Maybe there are," I said. "Maybe there are."

Chapter 30

At exactly two o'clock, the time we were closing up early, Adrian walked in the front door. He was carrying the sandwich board from the sidewalk and an armload of newspapers.

He looked around the store. It was empty, except for me and the dog.

"Good," he said, and he locked the door.

"Hello," I said coolly.

He dropped the newspapers on the counter in front of me. "We can start putting these on the windows."

"Really? That's all you have to say for yourself?"

He gave me a blank look. "Oh," he said. "Hello." He leaned forward across the counter to kiss me. I stepped back so I was out of reach.

He smiled. "I should have brought you a coffee. Is that why you're looking at me that way? I shouldn't have come empty-handed. What do you want? Mocha, right? I'll get it just how you like it, then we can get down to work."

"You think?"

He turned to leave then paused and handed me his phone. "Would you mind plugging this in? The battery died this morning. I've had the door locked at the new store all day because I didn't need people coming in and interrupting me." He rubbed his paint-flecked forehead with a paint-splattered hand. "It's been strange being cut off from the world. Did anything happen today that I should know about?"

"Lots of things," I said.

If he'd been cut off from the world, then he didn't know that Sunshine and Brittany and I had figured out he was dating all of us.

I hadn't anticipated that I'd be the one to break the news. How was I going to do it?

"You look beat," he said. He came around the counter, placed the phone in my hand, and kissed me while I was standing there in a daze. "I'll get you something to pep you up."

"Are you sure you want to do that?"

Grinning, he said, "What's gotten into you? Wait. Don't tell me. I'll be right back with some fuel to keep us going. It might be a late night. Do you like mustard and sauerkraut on your Reuben sandwich? Of course you do. It's not a Reuben without that."

He was back out the front door again and locking it behind him before I could say anything.

While he was next door getting food, I mentally rehearsed a big speech.

I hadn't worked out all the wording details—such as whether I'd call him *repugnant,* or *reprehensible,* or both—when he returned with the food.

As he was setting some meat on a paper plate in front of Cujo, he said, out of the blue, "I kissed Sunshine, and also Brittany."

"What?"

He patted Cujo, then stood up and looked me in the eyes. His icy-blue eyes were serious, and his long, angular features looked sharp under his slack facial tone.

"They set some ground rules for hanging out with me," he said. "There wasn't supposed to be any physical contact. But then, about two weeks ago, I kissed Brittany. It was dumb of me. Then, to even it out, I also kissed Sunshine." He looked down. "It was stupid and selfish."

"You kissed them," I said.

His shoulders rose up to his ears, and he gave me a sheepish look. "I think I only did it to try to make you jealous," he said. "Or maybe I wanted to kiss them. I don't know. But ever since last week, when I... showed you how to use the filing system, I haven't had any interest in either of them."

"You kissed them," I repeated. "Where?"

"Not at the roller skating rink," he said. "I only took you there, I swear."

"Um, what I meant was, where *on their body* did you kiss them?"

His eyes widened. "Just the mouth."

"Oh."

"Maybe a little tongue," he said.

I held up one hand. "That's enough detail."

"Are you mad?"

"I *was* mad," I said. "They came by this morning, and the way they were talking about it, I thought you'd done a lot more than kiss them. They said they had rules, and everybody was breaking them."

"I did break the ground rules," he said. "It was supposed to be zero body contact. Not even holding hands."

I was too stunned to say anything. I'd had several hours to stew on what I'd believed had happened. Several hours of getting more and more indignant. And now the rug of righteous fury had been yanked out from underneath me.

We stared at each other while Cujo slurped away noisily on his midafternoon snack.

"There's something else," Adrian said.

"I knew it," I said. "Another girl!"

"Sort of." He squinted. "Remember when your neighbor wanted me to kill that rat in his kitchen?"

"Yes. Mr. Galloway's rat."

"I couldn't kill it," Adrian said. "I put it in a plastic container and took it to the vet. The same one we took Cujo to. She amputated its injured leg. Don't worry—the rat's doing just fine on three legs. But I couldn't exactly release it into the world like that. So she's living in an old aquarium at my parents' house. My mother is not pleased."

A moment of silence passed.

I picked up the mocha he'd brought over and took a long drink.

Adrian said, "Her name is Munchies. Because she's always got the munchies. It should settle down once she's off the pain meds for her leg."

"You're harboring a fugitive," I said. "Mr. Galloway wanted that rat dead."

"She's just an innocent rat. You should see her little face." He lifted his hands to his cheeks and made a rat face.

"You're unbelievable," I said.

He dropped his hands and gave me a sad look. "I'm weak," he said. "I'm not much of a man, Peaches. If I were living in a hunter-gatherer tribe, they would run me out of the village for being a coward."

My emotions started to shift. Would I have killed the rat? Probably not. That was why I'd sent him over.

"I'm not much of a man," he repeated.

Now I felt sorry for him. We had put him in an uncomfortable situation. Kids who grew up on farms or went hunting with their family wouldn't have thought twice, but Adrian and I were city kids. We ate the McNuggets, but we'd never wrung a chicken's neck.

"You're still a man," I said. "I'm sure you would have been able to kill Mr. Galloway's rat if it had been a life or death situation."

"I don't know," he said. "I tried. I actually—"

I held up my hand. "Don't," I said. "I don't want to picture it. You're going to make me cry."

"You should see the way my father looks at me now. Like he can't believe I'm his son. My mom, too. I can see the disappointment on their faces. They know I'm a loser."

I came around the counter and put my hands on his cheeks. "You're not a loser," I said.

"But I keep screwing things up," he said. "I screw up everything."

"You're a human being. That's what humans do. Or at least that's what Nisha tells me. I wouldn't know, being perfect and everything."

"That's understandable," he said. "What with you being perfect and all."

I gave him a kiss and dropped my hands. "I'm glad you see things my way."

"I'm glad you can tolerate being around someone so much less perfect than you."

"It keeps me humble. It will help a lot once my modeling campaign goes live and everyone wants to *be* me."

He shook his head. "Nobody could ever be you."

"I hope they'll still try to become me by buying the overpriced underwear with my name on it."

"Your name? I thought you were just the model."

"There's a Peaches line named after me. The signature color is peach."

He sucked in a breath. "Of course it is," he said through gritted teeth.

"Don't be jealous," I said. "I had to share you with two other girls, and now you'll have to share me with the entire world."

He swallowed. "I hope the modeling thing works out, and that you're happy with whatever comes of it. Please tell me they paid you well."

"They paid me a lot of money. I wasn't sure about doing it, but the money helped me make up my mind."

"That's... how most bad business arrangements get started. You do know there is more to life than money, right?"

"Pfft. That's just something rich people say."

He frowned. "Rich people do tend to say that, but it doesn't make it any less true."

"Even so, I'd like to find out for myself," I said.

"And you shall."

He picked up his coffee and took a sip.

"You only kissed them?"

"On the mouth," he said. "With a little tongue."

"Where were your hands?"

"Honestly, I don't know."

"But it was just kissing?"

"Yes, and it was before you and I had that frank discussion in our boss's office about the filing system."

I took another sip of my mocha. I usually limited myself to one a day, so getting a midafternoon one was a real treat. Plus I'd needed it, after burning out my brain all day on righteous indignation and in-head speech rehearsing. What a day!

Adrian said, "I'm going to tell Brittany and Sunshine about us. I wanted to check with you first and make sure it was okay."

"You're a few hours too late," I said. "Sunshine came in here this morning on the pretense of seeing Cujo, then she grilled me like I was holding state secrets."

Adrian snorted.

"She'd make a good cop," I said. "You should have her talk to your father about a career change."

"She's pretty sharp," he said. "Brittany, not so much."

"Brittany needs to stay in her lane," I agreed. "But she is sweet."

"She is."

"And a good kisser?"

"No comment."

"Who was a better kisser?"

"You," he said.

"I mean between the two of them."

"There is no correct answer to that question," he said. "I plead the fifth."

"I bet it's Sunshine," I said.

He didn't comment.

"Maybe we'll have another wild house party and I'll find out for myself," I said.

Adrian raised an eyebrow.

"You won't be invited," I said.

He frowned.

"But I could take pictures," I said.

He shook his head and gestured to the food that was steaming on the counter. "Should we eat? It might be a long night."

I grabbed one of the foil packets and started unwrapping my Reuben. In addition to world-class donuts, Donut Joe's also made terrific hot sandwiches. Their takeout was just as good as the food over at Delilah's, minus the sassy attitude.

I sank my teeth into the salty, sour, juicy sandwich.

Adrian did the same with his.

I wiped my mouth. "I was going to dump you," I said. "I already told the other girls they could have you."

He pretended to be offended. "Am I just a piece of property to you women? Something to be bartered for over a game of poker?" He patted his chest. "I'm a real person, you know."

"A real person with a toothless dog and a three-legged rat, who lives with his parents and wears the same T-shirts he wore in high school."

He nodded. "That pretty much sums me up."

"You're okay," I said.

His blue eyes twinkled. "You're not so bad yourself, Peaches Monroe."

Chapter 31

I was ready to head in to work, so I went to see what was taking Nisha so long.

Since we needed extra help for the big move, and Nisha was currently between jobs, our operations manager had hired my roommate to act as casual labor for the transition.

I found her sitting on the floor of her bedroom with clothes spread out all around her. She was still in her underwear. She had her long, black, silky hair tied up in two buns.

"You look cute," I said. "We don't have an official Bookworm Books dress code, but you should probably wear pants."

"I don't have anything normal," she said glumly. "All I have is yoga wear and this breezy stuff that makes me look like I should be running a crystals-and-incense shop in Sedona."

"And this is suddenly a problem for you today?"
She pouted.

"You can wear your jeans that match mine," I said. "The ones that give me a panic attack whenever I try to put them on by accident."

She continued pouting. "With what?"

I picked up a sportswear top at random. "With this."

Her eyes lit up. "That would look nice. Thanks."

As she got dressed, I said, "Why are you even worried about what you're wearing? The store's closed, and we have newspapers all over the windows. Nobody's going to see you loading books into cardboard boxes."

"That's not true," she said. "You'll see me."

"What's really going on?"

"Noah said he might stop by to see how things are going."

"He'd better not. We're paying you to help us with the move, Nisha. Mr. Olivier won't approve of us paying you slightly more than minimum wage to have lousy sex with Noah on Mr. Olivier's office desk."

She sighed. "It is pretty lousy."

"Why do you keep doing it?"

"Haven't you ever eaten a stale donut?"

"Look at me," I said. "Do I look like the kind of girl who'd pass up a donut just because it has a little experience? Everyone knows they get better over time, when the edges crisp up. Not as much as mini marshmallows, though, which reach their peak after two years sitting in an opened bag."

"That's what it's like being with Noah," she said. "He's like crunchy marshmallows."

"Say no more." I gave her a hug. "Don't worry about it. We're young. It doesn't matter. If he makes you happy for now, that's good enough. All we have is right now. A giant asteroid could hit the planet any minute, and it won't matter."

She pulled away. "That's not as reassuring as you might think it is."

"Are you sure?"

She tilted her head to the side. "You're a mom," she said.

I looked down at myself. "That's a mean thing to say. Is it the jeans? I knew these were too high-waisted."

"It's your energy," she said. "I felt it just now. I always knew there was something calming about your energy, Peaches. It's because you've given birth. The things we experience leave a mark on us."

She waved her fingers at my aura. "I can see it now. You have goddess energy."

"Tell it to your crystals," I said. "Let's get to the bookstore before Adrian messes up everything."

She grabbed her purse and applied lipstick, and we left.

On the walk to the store, she pulled out her phone, looked over a screenful of messages, and said, "It looks like Adrian told the girls he picked you over them."

"I hope he didn't phrase it that way."

She read more and reported back, "Brittany says she still wants to keep the Quad Squad going. Sunshine says she's going to need a little time."

"Nisha, do *we* want to keep the Quad Squad going?"

She swished her lips from side to side. "It has been fun, having the old gang back together."

"You didn't tell Sunshine about Elliot, did you?"

She looked hurt. "Of course not. I wouldn't say a word about that to anyone. Why?"

"Just a feeling I get. Sorry I doubted you, but Sunshine is like a dog with a bone. The way she looks at me, and the way she talks, it's like she knows. Yesterday she accused me of having something going with Adrian for at least eight years. I've barely seen the guy until this summer."

"Everyone knows you two have a long and complicated history," Nisha said. "It's obvious to anyone with eyes."

I sighed. "I don't want it to be complicated anymore."

"Then just relax and let it unfold. A wise person once told me to take it easy and not think about the impending meteor strike that's going to end all life on the planet."

"Not *all* life on the planet," I said. "Just the humans. Everything else will be fine."

"How can you be so sure? Most mass extinctions aren't that selective."

"There will be an alien virus on the meteor that only affects humans," I said.

"Ah. That's a relief. I'd be upset if anything were to happen to the penguins."

"The penguins will be fine," I said.

We reached Baker Street then turned and headed toward the bookstore.

There was still time before we officially started our shift, so we popped into Donut Joe's to get mochas.

I saw a familiar face sitting over by the window, but it took a moment to place who the middle-aged man with the mustache was. I thought at first he might have been one of my father's work colleagues, but then it clicked. It was Bernard, Dalton Deangelo's butler.

He stood up when we made eye contact, and beckoned for me to come over.

I brought Nisha with me. They'd met once before, at the house. I reintroduced them in case they'd forgotten.

"It's English accent day at the donut shop," I joked. "I feel so left out."

Nisha and Bernard dove into the specifics of which regions of England their families had been from. It all flew over my head. If there wasn't a sauce named after an area, it all sounded made-up to me.

Bernard said to me, "I was hoping to speak to you for a moment in private, Ms. Monroe."

I replied, "Whatever you want to tell me, you can say it in front of Nisha. She's basically my butler. She knows me better than I know myself."

Nisha snorted at the idea of being my butler but let it go. She knew what I meant.

Rhonda brought our drinks over, and we sat with Bernard, squeezing in to fit all three of us around a table for two by the window.

Bernard rubbed his thick mustache nervously and cleared his throat.

"I, uh..." His face reddened, and he looked down.

"Let me guess," I said. "You gave me the script from Dalton's movie on purpose. It was no accident you gave a copy of *Waterfall* to me instead of my copy of the NDA."

He blinked at me. "How did you know?"

"Dalton figured it out," I said. "He mentioned that you don't make mistakes."

"Oh, but I do, ma'am," he said. "I should have given the script to you much sooner. I should have provided a copy when I drove you to Mr. Deangelo's Airstream. I anticipated that, given the thematic elements in the film, it would be better for you to know sooner rather than later."

"That might have put a damper on our evening at the Airstream," I said. "But what's done is done, and we can't do anything about the past. Life is not like a Hollywood script, where it can get a rewrite by a script doctor."

"If only," Bernard said.

Nisha sat watching quietly, sipping her beverage.

"What do you want from me?" I asked.

"I would very much like for you to give Mr. Deangelo a second chance."

"To do what?" I asked. "To completely rip my heart out and leave it in pieces?"

"Yes," Bernard said. "I mean no. Let me put it another way. Would you like to receive a designer gown to wear to a gala fundraiser? It's a charity for rescuing and relocating baby animals who have been orphaned during misadventure in the city."

I leaned back in my chair. "A designer gown and baby animals. You cunning fox, Bernard. You must know those are two things no woman could say no to."

"You'll go?" The butler gave me a hopeful look. "It would mean the world to me."

"No," I said.

He frowned. "Well, I didn't want to have to bring this up, but you did sign that agreement. You promised to do whatever was necessary to promote the film and Mr. Deangelo's career. The studio feels strongly that you should make an appearance tonight at the gala."

"How strongly?" I asked. "Are we talking about feelings, or lawyer stuff?"

Bernard couldn't look me in the eyes. "Lawyer stuff," he grumbled.

Nisha said, "You shouldn't have signed that contract without reading it."

"Thanks," I said. "Having my father tell me that repeatedly hadn't gotten through my thick skull yet."

"It's just a fundraiser," Bernard said. "It would make everyone happy." He met my eyes shyly. "Including me."

"Fine," I said. "I'll do it for you, Bernard. And also so I don't get sued. But mainly for you."

He held up both fists. "I'm chuffed."

I put my arm around Nisha. "Can my best friend come? It doesn't say anything in the NDA that I can't bring a friend."

He looked at Nisha. "I can't see why not," he said.

I asked, "Does she get a designer gown, too?"

"It can be arranged," he said. "It *shall* be arranged."

I looked at Nisha.

"Sure," she said. "I can't say no to a designer gown and baby animals."

I asked the butler, "Will your boss be there?"

"As your companion," Bernard said. "You'll need to be photographed together. And you'll be seated next to him at the dinner."

"I can handle those terms," I said. "You tell your boss there will be zero touchy-touchy of the peaches, or any other fruits, if you know what I mean. That goes double for Nisha."

Bernard blinked slowly. "I do understand," he said. "Thank you so much. You won't regret this. It's for a very good cause. The organization rehabilitates owls, coyotes, and raccoons, among other animals. You'll get to meet some of them at the event."

"I'll take a pass on the raccoons," I said. "But I could meet an owl."

Nisha said, "I'd love to meet any animals they have on hand."

Bernard said, "Shall I pick you both up at four o'clock at your private residence? I have the address."

"We've got to work until at least that time," I said.

"Then I'll pick you up here," he said. "That should give you just enough time to be fitted in the dresses and have your hair and makeup done professionally before the event begins."

"Why do I feel like Cinderella going to a ball?" I asked. "Are you my fairy godmother, Bernard? Does the car turn into a pumpkin at midnight?"

With a dry tone, he said, "Not until two o'clock, ma'am."

Chapter 32

An Hour Before the Fundraiser

Nisha gazed at herself in the mirror. We were in one of the hair and makeup trailers for Dalton's movie. Several of the cast members were attending the event, so everyone was getting prepared there.

Nisha couldn't take her eyes off herself. "I look like a Disney princess," she said. "Isn't it funny how life can turn on a dime? This morning, I was complaining about how I had nothing to wear. Now I'm in a designer gown. I generally try not to complain, but if that's what it takes to make the universe give you what you want, I'll give it a shot."

"I'm not sure the universe did anything," I said. "It was my stupidity, signing that stupid NDA without reading it."

"The universe has its ways." She used her phone to take yet another picture of herself.

The makeup artist putting the finishing touches on my face complimented me on my skin.

"I get that a lot," I said. "It must be genetics, because I don't do anything fancy."

The makeup artist finished and walked away.

Nisha leaned over and asked in a whisper, "What did Adrian say when he found out we were going out tonight with you-know-who?"

I rolled my eyes. "He made a gross comment about throwing his own gala party with Sunshine and Brittany, and serving one hot dog."

Nisha winced. "He didn't."

"He did," I said. "We've officially regressed beyond high school and all the way back to seventh grade."

"But what did he really say?"

"He told me to have fun."

"That was mature of him."

"And he told me to keep both feet on the floor at all times."

She gave me a serious look. "That's not bad advice."

I reached over and patted her arm. "That's why I have you with me as my chaperone, Grandma Nisha. You can stab Dalton Deangelo with your crochet needles if he gets too frisky."

She arched her beautifully made-up eyebrows. "It's not him I worry about." She looked around. "Where is he, anyway?"

"Still shooting a scene," I said. "Bernard might have to make two trips. One of the PAs told me when you were in the washroom. He's shooting a scene with the actress who plays Harper. She's not coming to the fundraiser. The PA told me the studio didn't want"—I made air quotes—"*two of us* there at the same time, pulling focus."

Nisha's jaw dropped. "Two of you? As in... two curvy blondes?"

"Yeah," I said. "When I heard that, I just about walked out in protest, but you were having so much fun, and I thought, who cares? I am what I am. Honestly, I don't want some Hollywood doppelganger pulling focus from me."

Nisha gave me a sad look. "We can both walk out of here right now. You don't have to do this for me."

"Think of the owls," I said. "We're doing it for the owls."

She nodded.

"Plus so I don't get sued," I said.

"And the swag bags," she added. "I do like the idea of getting a swag bag."

"There'd better not be any raccoons in my swag bag."

She smiled. "How are you feeling?"

I looked around the hair and makeup trailer. "Excited," I said. "This is fun. I enjoyed it in LA for the photo shoot, and I still love it. I can see how people get swept up in all the trappings of fame."

"It is exciting," Nisha said. "I'm sure it gets old when this is your regular life every day, but it's a treat to get to experience it for a while."

"The only thing missing from tonight is Mitchell," I said. "I wish you could have met him. He's so much fun. You two would get along."

"Maybe I could go with you the next time you fly to LA. I could be your chaperone and make sure you don't get into trouble with the other underwear models."

"You could try," I said, waggling my eyebrows. "Maybe we could both get into trouble together."

"Deal." She offered me her pinkie, and we did a pinkie swear.

There was a tap on the door of the trailer. Bernard was ready to drive us to the fundraiser.

I suspected Dalton might be hiding in the back of the car, behind the tinted windows, but the car was empty.

I got into the empty back seat.

Bernard said, "Mr. Deangelo is taking alternate transportation. He'll meet us there, and he shouldn't be too much longer."

Nisha slid into the back seat beside me, careful not to wrinkle her fancy dress.

Bernard drove us to the fundraiser. It was being held at the Cedars, the same exclusive country club where Dalton had accompanied me to my cousin Tina's wedding reception.

When we reached the Cedars, Bernard stopped the car but didn't jump out to open the door for us.

I asked, "Is there a problem?"

"No problem, ma'am," he said. "We'll wait in the car until the other vehicle arrives with Mr. Deangelo."

"Why?"

Bernard explained patiently, "The whole point of a public appearance together is so that you'll be seen together. Some photography will happen upon entering the building."

"Can't they just use the pictures of us sitting at the table together?"

He didn't turn back to make eye contact. "Walking in together was Mr. Deangelo's request," he said. "Arriving together makes more of a statement than simply being seen together."

"You tricked me," I said.

Haughtily, he replied, "I did not."

I turned to Nisha. "You were there. Did it sound like tonight was supposed to look like we were on a date?"

Nisha said, "I don't know, Peaches. It all happened so fast. When you two were talking, I was mostly thinking about getting a maple cream eclair."

"Some chaperone you are," I said to her.

She shrugged. "Does it matter?"

"Of course it matters," I said. "I told Adrian I was going to this wild animal thing because of my modeling obligations. If it's going to look like I'm dating Dalton, that's different."

"But I'm here," she said. "I promise to spoil the mood if it gets too romantic."

"If I was in the market for a mood spoiler, I would have brought Elliot," I said. "Or my parents."

She looked down at my dress, a sapphire-blue number that hugged my curves.

"Just relax and enjoy looking gorgeous," she said. "This is like prom, but better."

"Let's hope it doesn't end like prom," I said.

"Ugh, prom." Nisha made a gagging face.

On prom night, my date had been a neighbor boy who'd put the moves on me, only to wind up being intimate with the cushions of a leather couch, all the while believing he was rocking my world. Not one of my finest moments.

Nisha's date that night had been a perfect gentleman, right up until he snuck off to make out with not one but two other boys. The next day, all three of the boys had independently claimed that they'd enjoyed some degree of intimacy with Nisha. Rumors flew. A week later, the scandal had blown over, but Nisha—and her family—had been horrified. Her parents had even started up with the whole arranged marriage thing. Luckily for Nisha, they'd eventually let it go once the truth about that night came out.

We giggled about prom while we waited.

After twenty minutes, another vehicle pulled up beside us. Dalton Deangelo jumped out.

My breath caught in my chest.

He was wearing a tuxedo. Like the one Sir Drake Cheshire had worn to the party where he'd defeated the king of the zombies in a sword duel.

Dalton's dark hair flopped in the summer breeze. The sun glinted off his pearly teeth. His emerald-green eyes sparkled. He looked like an image that had been heavily retouched and filtered, except that wasn't possible, because this was real life.

Nisha leaned in and whispered, "I do see the appeal."

I whispered back, "Looks aren't everything."

"Try to keep your mind on Adrian."

"Who?" I was joking, but also not joking.

Bernard opened our door, and we stepped out.

Dalton beamed. "Nisha! I'm so glad you made it. I've missed seeing you. How are things at the yoga studio?"

"I quit that job," she said. "I'm currently unemployed."

"Not exactly," I said. "She's helping out with the bookstore. I don't know if you heard the news, but we're moving to a smaller location to save money."

Dalton looked directly at me. Time stopped. I forgot what I'd been talking about.

"Thank you for coming tonight," he said. "It means a lot to me."

"I'm only here so I don't get sued. And also for the baby animals. Not the raccoons, but definitely the owls."

He blinked. "The what?"

Nisha turned to me and said, "He probably doesn't know what this fundraiser is for." She looked at him. "Isn't that right? You probably go to these things all the time, and they all blend together."

He looked around to make sure nobody was within listening range, then said, "I have no idea what this thing is for. I put on my tuxedo when they tell me to. As long as there's food, I'm happy enough." He looked me in the eyes again, taking away whatever breath I'd managed to inhale. "And with two lovely ladies as my companions, I couldn't be happier."

He held out his arms for us to each take one.

"There's something different about your energy," Nisha said. "You seem calmer."

We took his arms and started walking toward the Cedars' entrance. A throng of photographers awaited.

Dalton said to Nisha, "The last time you saw me, I was not at my best."

She said, "It was at the house party, when Adrian Stromquist was mocking your movie script. Peaches was yelling at you for playing your David character with her and using her for research."

His jaw stiffened. "Not a good evening for me, or for anyone involved," he said. "I'm glad I got out of your house before the attack set in. You were probably back to singing karaoke by the time I was admitted to the hospital and hooked up to a heart monitor."

I stopped in my tracks. "What? Are you saying Adrian and I gave you a heart attack?"

"Panic attack," he said softly, mindful of the photographers up ahead. "I've had them before, but they've been getting worse lately."

Nisha said, "I could help you with that. There are breathing techniques, and things you can do with your eyes. The diaphragm is a two-way tool for communicating with the autonomic system. Plus there are visualizations you can try, like surrounding yourself in white light, and..." She trailed off and glanced away, embarrassed. "It's stupid. I know. I'm the weirdo who's into all the woo-woo stuff. You can dress me up, but I'm still Nisha Papadum who did stuff with three guys at prom. Allegedly."

Dalton dropped my arm and turned to face Nisha. I couldn't see his expression, but he was looking into her eyes with absolute focus.

"Don't ever apologize for who you are," he said to my best friend. "And don't ever be ashamed of trying to help people. Those are the only two things in this world that are worth doing. Being yourself, and helping others.”

“Okay,” she said, nodding.

“And I thought your last name was Patel?”

She grinned. “The kids in school called me Nisha Papadum.”

He said, “The kids in school called me a lot of bad names. They turned Deangelo into McDevil, and they changed my first name into something unmentionable. The first letters are D-I-L.”

Nisha mouthed the full name then said, “That’s awful.”

“Thanks to them, I got my first taste of acting,” he said. “I acted like it didn’t bother me.”

“Aww.” She gave him a pity face. “That must have been terrible.”

“I’m working through it,” he said. “As for the anxiety techniques, I have been learning some things. It’s hard, though. Intense anxiety makes me lock up completely. I’m not like some people, who can keep breathing and talking no matter what.” He glanced back at me.

“It’s true,” I said. “I’m very calm under pressure.”

Nisha said, “That might be why you’re drawn to Peaches. Her nervous system is communicating with yours on a quantum level. Being around her calms you down.”

I held up my hand. “Are you saying I’m some sort of therapy dog for Dalton?”

“Something like that,” Nisha said.

He turned to me, grinning. “Peaches is more of a therapy *cat*,” he said. “Cats are independent and uncontrollable.”

“Meow,” I said.

Nisha patted Dalton on the shoulder. “You make a pretty good therapy cat yourself, Dalton. I was nervous about going in there, but I think I'll be just fine on your arm."

He looked at me expectantly.

"Enough chitchat," I said as I took his other arm. "Let's get in there before they run out of champagne."

Chapter 33

The fundraiser was glamorous but also fun.

Nisha stood off to the side while I had my photograph taken with the rescue animals. I was holding a tiny, squirmy raccoon while an owl supervised wisely from its perch.

"Look at you, cuddling a raccoon," Nisha said, shaking her head. "I never thought I'd see the day." She turned to the animal assistant and explained, "She's terrified of raccoons."

"Not this one," I said. "Look at its little itty bitty paws! They're like teeny weeny hands in black gloves!"

"You don't have to tell me," Nisha said. "I've always liked raccoons."

I changed my grip on the little squirmer to keep it from scaling my bare shoulder and scratching me.

I planned to hand the baby animal back to the assistant, but the raccoon—a male—had other plans. He went for a nosedive, taking shelter in my cleavage.

"Look at that," I said. Its body disappeared, and only its striped tail remained visible. "Right between the peaches."

The photographer snapped away like a maniac.

The animal assistant apologized and escorted me to a private space behind a screen where I could retrieve the little rascal.

"That's a new one," I said to the assistant. "Guys are always trying to put their faces in there, but never their whole body."

"It happens a lot," the young woman said, putting the baby raccoon back into a basket with a heating pad. "Whenever we take the babies to one of these galas, someone gets an animal inside their clothes, someone has their toupee pulled off, and someone gets pooped on."

"When you put it that way, I'm glad I wasn't pooped on."

She pointed to a table of cleaning products and paper towels. "We come prepared."

"Good to know," I said. "Will you be here all evening? I can be a messy eater."

The assistant grinned. "You can come see me anytime." She added suggestively, "For absolutely anything."

I thanked her, adjusted the top of my sapphire-blue dress, and returned to the photography area just in time to see an older man getting his toupee yanked off by the owl.

Nisha and I walked away, holding onto our giggles until we were at a safe distance.

She wiped a tear from her eye. "When that raccoon took a header into your chest, I nearly lost it."

"Can't say I blame the little guy," I said. "I think the animal assistant was hitting on me." I adjusted my cleavage. "My sweater puppies have never looked better." I looked over at her cleavage, which was also impressive. "Yours, too."

She covered the center of her chest. "I'd better keep guard over myself, or they'll have to frisk me for baby animals on the way out." She gave me a serious look. "Are you still okay being here?"

"Of course. Why wouldn't I?"

"Dalton keeps making those sexy eyes at you."

"That's just how his face looks."

"Not exactly," she said. "He's very attractive, in a wildly implausible way, but the way he looks at you is different from how he looks at other people."

"It must be all the quantum stuff with our energy chakras or whatever, like you said."

"I know you're joking, but there's always more going on than what we see with our eyes."

The left side of my face suddenly felt warm, like a spotlight was on it. I turned and immediately made eye contact with Dalton Deangelo. The handsome actor was casually holding a conversation with some other men in tuxedos. Dalton had a black bird on his shoulder. Both the actor and the bird looked comfortable with the arrangement.

Dalton raised his glass of champagne at me and winked.

I turned back to Nisha. "He is attractive in a wildly implausible way."

"And he looks at you the way you look at whipped cream."

"Speaking of whipped cream, when's the last time we ate?"

"It's been hours," she said. "I'm starving. When they do finally ring the dinner bell, I'm liable to eat until I bust the seams on this borrowed dress."

"Don't do that," I said. "It's yours, Nisha. They said we could keep the dresses."

She gave me a dismayed look. "That's nice, but when would I ever wear this again?"

"Mitchell says having great clothes in your closet means you'll find great things to do in them." I glanced around at the crowd. "It's too bad he's not here. He'd love this."

There was a shift in the noise in the ballroom. The event's announcer invited everyone to take their seats for the dinner service.

The urgency with which everyone was moving reminded me of my cousin's wedding. We'd been in the same ballroom, though that had been a buffet dinner and tonight we would have our food brought to us in courses.

Nisha and I made our way over to our assigned table. We were seated with Dalton and a few of his colleagues from the movie he was shooting in town.

Dalton joined us. He reached for my leg under the table and gave it a reassuring squeeze. I should have swatted his hand away but didn't. He leaned over and whispered, "I'm so sorry you have to endure this painfully dull dinner."

"Are you joking? I'm having a great time. I had a baby raccoon crawl into my dress. Right here." I pointed at my cleavage.

He looked down and licked his lips. "Can't say I blame him. I'd take shelter in there myself, if I could."

"You could try," I said.

Nisha, who was seated on the other side of Dalton, cleared her throat and gave us both a stern look.

Dalton smiled and leaned back. "I thought hanging out with one of you girls was fun, but both of you together are certainly interesting. Nisha, how do you feel about hiking? And hot springs?"

"I love hiking," she said. "If we're going to trespass, we should wear wide-brimmed hats to conceal our identities."

He laughed. "Now we're talking."

He turned to me and said, "Thanks so much for coming tonight."

"I couldn't say no," I said. "Thanks to that stupid NDA."

"You are as good for my nerves as you are for my public image," Dalton said. "And so is your mom. Everyone loved the pictures of us shopping at the toy store. Everyone wants to know who Elliot is."

I pulled back. "Leave him out of this. He's just a little kid."

Dalton's expression went serious. "Understood," he said coolly. "If we go on any more shopping trips, I'll wear a wide-brimmed hat and make sure nobody recognizes me." He took a sip of his champagne. "How old were you when Elliot came along?"

"Fifteen."

"That must have been quite the lifestyle change for you."

"What do you mean?"

"You were an only child, like me. You had your parents to yourself, and then you didn't."

"I suppose that part was weird." I picked up my champagne and tossed it back. "What about you? Did your parents ever think about having more kids?"

"They tried," he said. "That was when they found out my father's little swimmers didn't work." He looked down. "That was when my father figured it all out."

He meant that his father had learned of his mother's affair with actor Jocko Ranger.

"I'm so sorry," I said. "I thought you told me you didn't know about that until your mother was quite ill?"

"I didn't know until then," he said. "But my father knew for a long time. It actually explains a lot." He continued looking down. The tendons on his neck flexed and stood out. "It's not fair for a kid to not know where he comes from."

"Your mother was only doing what she thought was for the best," I said.

His nostrils flared. He turned to me, his emerald-green eyes blazing. "How would you know?"

I didn't have an answer I could tell him.

"People always make excuses for other people," he said. "They always try to talk you out of how you feel."

I held up my hands. "That's not what I meant to do."

He looked away, adjusted the tilt of his head, then turned back to me. His eyes were no longer blazing. He looked tired. There were dark circles under those gorgeous eyes of his. I hadn't noticed how exhausted and drawn he looked until he'd stopped smiling.

"You're a good person, Peaches. I shouldn't have snapped at you. Can you forgive me?" He made puppy-dog eyes.

"That was nothing," I said. "We were just talking about stuff. If we're going to be friends or whatever, a bit of friction is going to happen."

His eyes twinkled. "You want to be friends, *or whatever*?"

"Sure. We might as well be on good terms, if we're going to be doing publicity stuff together."

He raised an eyebrow.

The waiter brought our first appetizer, a seafood dish. An extremely tiny seafood dish.

"I've sneezed bigger portions," I said to Dalton. "Please tell me there's more food coming."

The waiter, who was still standing behind me, said, "There will be eight more courses, ma'am."

I looked up at him. "Are they all this size?"

He gave me a genuine smile. "No, ma'am. They get better. You may not have room for dessert."

I said, "Wanna bet?"

The waiter had started to laugh as he left.

Dalton reached over and squeezed my leg again. "You make even the dullest events fun, Peaches. Where have you been all my life?"

"Mostly standing on chairs, trying to fall into the arms of unsuspecting men."

"I knew it." He picked up his fork. With the skill of a surgeon, he portioned off one third of the microscopic seafood appetizer.

I mashed mine with the back of my fork so I didn't waste any.

The next course was slightly larger. At least it was tasty.

Whenever I looked up, at least two of the other people seated at our table had their eyes on my chest. I had to keep checking to make sure a baby raccoon wasn't hiding in there again.

By the fifth course, I was simply enjoying myself.

Nisha was telling Dalton about her wacky spells, and how they worked to align a person's focus. She told him how she'd cast a love spell on me the day before he and I had met.

"I knew it," he said. "There were definitely cosmic forces at work."

"Just me," Nisha said proudly.

The three of us continued joking around, teasing Nisha about her beliefs, and talking about the food on offer.

When the waiter brought the final course, a dessert trio, he congratulated me on having won our bet.

I asked him, "When do you get to eat? You must be starving."

He seemed surprised by my question. "The chef has some items under a heat lamp. I'll take my meal break after the coffee service."

"Do you get dessert? Is there one of these waiting for you?" I pointed to my dessert.

"Probably not," he said, wrinkling his nose. "The kitchen staff usually makes short work of them before we get back there. Which is a shame, because the chocolate cherry cheesecake is my favorite."

"Come here." I gestured for the waiter to lean down, as though I was about to tell him a secret.

I used a clean fork and stabbed the cheesecake, then brought it to the waiter's mouth.

"Choo choo," I said, the way I used to say it to Elliot when I helped my mother feed him.

The waiter opened his mouth and ate the cheesecake. We shared a giggle, and then he walked away.

I looked over at Dalton, who was staring at me.

"You are such a naughty girl," he said. "You're a bad influence on everyone, aren't you? Here I was blaming myself for the trouble I got us into, but it was always you. You're a trouble magnet."

"It was just a bit of cheesecake," I said. "I've worked restaurant jobs. I know what it's like to make sure everyone else is taken care of while you're dying for a bite."

Dalton said, "I've worked those jobs, too. Before I got my break. I never once had a customer feed me cheesecake, or anything else for that matter, off their plate. Let alone a customer as cute as you." He glanced in the direction the waiter had left. "Be careful. You heard the animal rescue spokesperson. If you feed a wild creature, it may follow you home and demand more."

"You're the only wild creature I worry about." I pointed to his plate. "Are you going to eat that?"

"You know I won't," he said.

I reached over and took his plate.

He gave me a puzzled look. "Did you give your cheesecake away because you knew you'd be getting mine?"

"Yes. And also because I'm nice."

"You are nice. Nice to look at." He leaned over and looked down my dress. "Where did you say that raccoon went?"

I pushed him back. "Behave yourself. I'm only here as a friend, and to avoid legal action. I'm your... what did we call it? I'm your *therapy cat*."

"My therapy cat," he agreed.

I finished eating his dessert, and the waiter brought coffee and tea.

Nisha leaned over and said, "Don't look now, but something's happening over there."

Despite her warning, we both looked.

At one of the other tables, a group of people were crowded around a phone, watching something—a video. There was audio of people shouting, but I couldn't make out the words.

I did notice, however, that the people watching the video kept talking furtively to each other and glancing over at our table. At Dalton, specifically.

The actor leaned over and whispered to me, "Is it just my paranoia, or are they talking about me?"

"They do seem to be talking about you," I said. "Is this something that happens all the time?"

"Not quite like this," he said. "There must be something new on the internet about me."

Bernard suddenly appeared behind Dalton's chair. He put a hand on Dalton's shoulder. "Sir, we should leave now."

"Not so fast," Dalton said. "I haven't done anything wrong. I'm an actor, not a criminal."

Bernard said, "I strongly suggest we leave at once, sir."

Dalton turned to Nisha. "Are you girls ready to leave? Would that be okay? Bernard can overreact sometimes, but his heart's in the right place."

"Sir," Bernard said, more strongly.

"Okay, okay," Dalton said.

He got up.

As he stood, a woman from another table came over and got right into his face.

"You're a pig," she said. "Just like your father, Jocko Ranger."

Dalton's jaw dropped.

The woman had just outed him as Jocko Ranger's son. That was a first, as far as I knew.

I looked over at Nisha, who was staring at me, wide-eyed. I had told my mother about Dalton's father, but not my roommate. Nisha was as stunned as the rest of the people present at the fundraiser.

Dalton didn't respond to the woman.

She said, "Don't you have anything to say for yourself?"

He dropped his gaze and attempted to walk around her.

"Pig," the woman said again, and she threw her drink in his face.

Dalton froze. The drink had been coffee—not scalding hot, thankfully—and it dribbled down his face and stained his tuxedo.

Then he started breathing. His breath was high in his chest, and rapid.

As I watched in stunned silence, his breathing got faster and faster. He was hyperventilating.

Bernard leaned over to me and said, "Find a paper bag and meet me in the car."

Then he grabbed Dalton by the arm and dragged him out of the ballroom at top speed.

By this point, the entire crowd gathered in the ballroom had figured out something was going on. There was an uproar of voices and chaos everywhere.

I grabbed Nisha by the hand, and we darted through the crowd, straight into the kitchen.

I found our friendly waiter, asked him for a paper bag, and he gave us a stack of bags, no questions asked.

We thanked him and ran out to the car.

The doors were closed. We knocked on the back door's window.

The window rolled down. Bernard took the paper bags, thanked me, and rolled the window back up again.

Nisha and I stood in our fancy cocktail dresses next to the car, waiting to see if Dalton would be okay.

I hadn't considered looking on the internet to find out what exactly had set off the drink-tossing woman, but Nisha did.

She did a search on her phone and reported back to me, "This might be a big deal." She looked up at me. "Is Dalton really Jocko Ranger's illegitimate son?"

"Yes." There was no point now in denying it.

"Peaches, I'm sorry I have to ask you this, but did Jocko Ranger sleep with your mother?"

"Is that what the internet is saying?"

"It's what *Jocko* is saying."

"In that case, yes."

Nisha shook her head. "The internet is very upset that Dalton is having an intimate relationship with his half-sister."

"With Josie Ranger?"

"No. With you."

"But I'm not his half-sister. My father is Peter Monroe. My mother *did* have a fling with Jocko, but it was several years before I was born. It was around the time Dalton was conceived, and he's a few years older than me, by anyone's account."

She wrinkled her nose. "I believe you. That's not nearly as scandalous, if you aren't related by blood. So, three guesses what the internet and Jocko Ranger believe. Three guesses, and the first two don't count."

"That's ridiculous," I said. "They can't believe something that's not true. Do I look twenty-seven?"

Nisha raised an eyebrow at me.

"Ugh," I said.

She frowned at her phone a bit more. "This explains what happened. It looks like Jocko saw the photos of Dalton in the toy store with your mother, and he recognized your mom. Then he came up with some crazy story about how Dalton was only dating you as some sort of plot to humiliate him. Jocko decided to get ahead of the scandal."

"What a narcissist! This has nothing to do with him!"

"He is an actor," Nisha said.

"They're not all narcissists, but Jocko Ranger is." I shook my head. "I can't believe Dalton stood up for that man."

"Blood is thicker than water."

"This is ridiculous," I said. "The internet can't believe something that's so obviously not true."

She raised her eyebrow.

"Ugh," I said again.

Another car pulled up next to us. The driver got out and introduced himself as being with the studio. He said he would drive us home.

Nisha said to me, "I guess our job here is done. We've fulfilled your legal obligations." She headed toward the other car. "Are you coming, Peaches?"

I was still standing next to Dalton's car. My feet refused to move.

"I should wait and see if he's okay," I said.

"He's got Bernard. What good are you doing to do?"

I shrugged.

"All that talk about you being his therapy cat—it was just a joke," Nisha said. "You don't have any obligation, legal or otherwise, to do anything for him tonight."

"I know."

"But you want to get in that car with him, don't you?"

I nodded.

She shivered and crossed her arms over her chest. "What about Adrian? If you get in that car with Dalton, you know he won't be happy."

"Put it on the long list of things that don't make Adrian happy," I said.

"You should get in this car with me and come home. We had our fun night out. We got to play Cinderella at the ball. Now it's midnight, and things are about to turn into pumpkins."

"It's barely nine o'clock."

"You know what I mean." She took in a deep breath and gradually relaxed her arms. "Who am I kidding? You're not going to do what I say is best for you. Peaches Monroe is her own boss, and she takes instructions from no one, even if it's for her own good."

"I love you," I said.

"I love you, too," she said.

Then she got into the car, waved goodbye, and left.

I tapped on the window of Dalton's car.

The door opened.

The end of Book 2, Whole Lotta Peaches.

To be continued in Book 3, Everything is Peaches by
Angie Pepper